THE COMFY-COZY NIHILIST

a handbook of dark fiction

NATHAN D. LUDWIG

Praise For LOVE POTION #666 - Now Available From
D&T Publishing

"A rollicking journey that carries all the fun of a hit grindhouse novel. Ludwig knows how to keep readers entertained!"
- Samantha Kolesnik, author of True Crime and Waif

"Loaded with guns, gore, and grime. I loved it!"
- Mike Lombardo, director of I'm Dreaming of a White Doomsday and author of Please Don't Tap on the Glass

"Great plot, great characters, great dialogue (to be expected from Nathan), and everyone knows how much I love a good one-liner. Plenty of them here to entertain, all wrapped up with a nasty grindhouse feel to proceedings."
- Mark Towse, author of Nana, Crows, and One Last Shinding

"Love Potion #666 is the kind of book that you want to get into a barfight with… and then make out with afterwards."
- Jaysen Buterin, director of Kill Giggles

"Love Potion #666 is a bona fide pulp horror masterpiece."
- Ryan Imhoff, director of Fresh Hell

"…a high speed, super-fun, late-night cable movie on acid."
- Aaron S. Barrocas, award-winning screenwriter and director of Half-Cocked & Sitting Duck

"Get ready for a ride that will leave you disgusted and laughing in the end!"
- Chad Farmer, author of Earth Truckers Are Easy and Devil Won't Let Me Be

"A hilariously wild and bloody ride. I loved every single insane sequence!"
- *Evan Baughfman, author of The Emaciated Man and Vanishing of the 7th Grade*

"I had such a good time with this book. It is loaded with loveable characters who are terrible people who find themselves in all sorts of ridiculous situations chock full of sex, violence, and hilarity."
- *Jeff Frumess, podcaster and director of Romeo's Distress and Gouge Away*

"This is a wild, insane, fast-paced road trip (chase?) with zombies and sex cocaine - how can you go wrong?"
- *Todd Densmore, director of Blue and Cardinal*

"I loved this book! It's gory, funny, fast-paced, intelligently done, and has some of the best dialogue. Definitely recommend!"
- *R.J. Benetti, author of The Slappening & Santa Muerte Claus*

RECOMMENDED FILM LIST

ARSENIC & OLD LACE (1944)

AUGUST: OSAGE COUNTY (2013)

FOUR LIONS (2010)

FRANK (2014)

KILL LIST (2011)

KILLERS (2014) (this is not the Ashton Kutcher/Katherine Heigl movie)

MARTYRS (2008)

MULTIPLICITY (1996)

R100 (2013)

RUBBER (2010)

SÉANCE (2000)

SOUND OF NOISE (2011)

TALK RADIO (1988)

WEEKEND AT BERNIE'S (1989)

WAKE IN FRIGHT (1971)

For Peckinpah, S. Leone, Astron-6, Python, Tarantino, M. Harron, Palahniuk, Poe, Leonard, Zahler, Miike, Sono, D. Siegel, Dupieux, K. Link, M. Mann, Zevon, Cohens Leonard & Larry, McCarthy, Stone, Easton Ellis, Zombie, Doom, Silverstein, D. Lynch, Carpenter, Kesey, Craven, Linnell & Flansburgh, K. Bush, Matsumoto H., Cronenberg, Verhoeven, B. Gibbons, J. Eisener, R. Dahl, and Kurosawa K.

They're all in here somewhere…

STORIES...

"Told my little Pollyanna

There's a place for you and me

We'll go down to Transverse City

Life is cheap and death is free"

~Transverse City

"I went walking through the wasted city

Started thinking about entropy

Smelled the wind from the ruined river

Went home to watch TV"

~Run Straight Down

~Warren Zevon, Transverse City (1987)

INTRO...

I can hear you mouthing the words right now.

"Who the fuck is Nathan D. Ludwig and why does he have a collection?"

Regardless of whether you've heard of me or not, I've got stories to tell, and I don't have a lot of time to waste anymore. I'm just getting down to it without any pretense at this point in my life. You're welcome to join me as I attempt whatever it is I'm doing in these pages.

I published my first novel this year and that was a big deal for me. Just the sheer act of getting it done and getting it out there is a nice feeling. It's called *Love Potion #666* and it's pretty swell if I do say so myself. If you like grindhouse action/horror stuff and violent 90s cult classic films, you'll be in hog heaven.

But that's neither here nor there with the book you have in your hands right now. *The Comfy-Cozy Nihilist* is indeed a collection of weird, dark, funny, fucked-up short stories that all come from different places in my head. They also have different origin stories, as well. Some started as screenplays, some began as submissions to open calls at various presses, and some were created just for this here occasion.

Secret sex exhibitions, decadent primetime programming, the hypocritical relationship between belief and skepticism, disingenuous altruism, the terrifying patience of a father's vengeance, the drudgery of order in service to chaos, the cancer that is social media, believing in your own bullshit, and so much more lurk within these pages.

And after (or during) reading, some of you will realize (or already know) what I have known for a while now.

I envy those who lie to themselves with promises of paradise and providence. I really do. It must make existence that much more tolerable.

I seriously want you to enjoy these stories. They each come from a piece of truth buried deep within me. The stuff we usually don't say out loud or online; places where there's no room for nuance or honesty. Not like here, on the page. We can't hide from each other here.

You don't have to like me. You just need to read honestly.

Please enjoy.

FUCK FANGSGIVING

Mama's breastplate was damn near impossible to break through. Also, my stake sucked ass. So, I yelled at Dom to cut her fucking head off just as the sun finished setting on our family's decrepit excuse for a farm.

His ax did not suck ass. Lopped the bitch's head clean off and sent it rolling across the living room floor akin to a hairy watermelon on the loose. The THWUMP it kept on making made me wanna hurl. Even moreso than the damn decapitation itself.

"What's wrong with your stake all of a sudden?"

I know he meant it as a genuine question, and I tried mighty hard to answer accordingly but all I could muster was "The fuck's that supposed to mean?"

"Got a few more in the truck. Want me to get you one?"

"If it ain't too much trouble on ya," I said with a condescending smile. Why was I being such an asshole?

Might've had something to do with our family turning into a blessed-ass nest of vampires and the fact they lured us back home from college with the promise of a bona fide Russo Family Thanksgiving dinner. They were downright legendary. But nah, they just wanted to suck us dry and burn our bodies. It pissed me off proper just thinking about it. Why couldn't *we* be vampires too? The fuck was the deal with that? What, *we're* not good enough? Ain't vampire material? They all had to die. Fuck 'em.

My brother Dom's always been my best friend. Even when we didn't want to *be* best friends. We were both dreamers in a family chock full of working stiffs. So that made us weirdos. Layabouts. Malingerers. Any excuse to wave off our ambition as unnatural so they could go back to their bitter drudgery. We were set to inherit that drudgery, but we had other plans.

Dom got a scholarship for wrestling, and I managed to get fully funded for a major in Fine Art thanks to our Uncle Tolliver. Mama's older brother. Another involuntary oddball of the family. He owned a pawn shop in Tuscaloosa. Had a boatload of money invested in porn production. Art is art, I guess. And I wasn't going to turn down a chance to get out of Assfuck, Texas. Needless to say, Tolliver wasn't welcome at any Russo family events. Not a one. It made accepting all that money even sweeter. Pleasurable, even.

As much as we'd said we were gonna go our separate ways for college, we ended up in the same damn place. University of Arizona. Can you believe that shit? We applied to a handful of schools and U of A was the only one that accepted either one of us. Stuck together again. I had my heart set on Arizona State. Suited my personality down to the ground. I don't think Dom cared either way. We'd be away from Mama. Away from the clan. That's all that mattered in his book. Mine too, if I'm being all the way honest.

Neither one of us were exactly of the popular kind. Dom was the ultimate introvert. But his size and objectively handsome features kept would-be bullies away. Kids just plain ignored him.

I, on the other hand, had always been prime fodder for mean girls. I was never skinny per se, but I wasn't outright fat, neither. I had what I thought were pretty nice hips and found out soon the popular girls - the Twigs we called 'em - *hated* nice hips. Anything shapely. They wanted to kill it all with fire. Boys pretty much stayed away from me due to the Dom factor. Girls, too. They couldn't make heads nor tails outta neither one of us. So that was my high school existence in a lonely, hateful nutshell.

Naturally then, we gravitated toward each other. Support. Commiseration. The usual. Our excuse was always biding time in each other's company until we could find real friends. Real friends that never came. Looking back, I guess they were scared of us? Dom had a few dates, but nothing ever came of it. Had nothing to do with me, I swear.

We weren't gonna tell Mama. No fucking way. Since we were Irish twins as it were, we both turned eighteen our senior year so there wasn't shit she could do about it. We'd just quietly slip away one August night and never come back.

At least, that's what we thought would happen.

After we'd graduated, over summer break, our family started turning into fuckin' vampires.

It all technically started when Uncle Frank, Daddy's twin brother, dropped dead at Sunday spaghetti dinner. Just fell over face first into a plate of his own special recipe of sauce and meatballs. No last words. Just a look of utter surprise. And terror. Doc said his heart exploded. Fucking *exploded*, he said. Not a heart attack. Not a stroke. Heart *explosion*. Guess that's what a degree from El Centro gets you. I mean, I know it's a real thing, but fuck-a-duck could you have a better bedside manner for fuck's sake?

Anyways, from then on, spaghetti dinners on Sundays never happened again. You'd think they'd keep on even stronger to honor Uncle Frank's memory and what not. Nope. Just stopped colder than Mama's icebox in January. Mama *insisted*. So did Daddy. And they never agreed on nothin'. *Ever*.

Once our uncle and spaghetti dinners went away, so did anything that happened before sundown. Our folks slept in late, almost past sunset. Never went outside 'til well after dusk. Smoked more. Drank more. Late night card games and dancin' in the barn all hours of the night right up on dawn's blessed ass crack. Then all was quiet again. Couldn't figure it out for the life of me.

Then, few weeks before we were fixin' to make our escape, I found something. Out behind the barn. Something—

"That you, kids? The hell is the noise about? Where's Ellie?"

Fuck. Grandpa Dean. Come to check on Mama. And dinner, no doubt. The utter glutton.

We'd managed to cut off Mama's head before she could finish stuffin' the turkey. I'm sure he was hobbling in to criticize her and peck at the breadcrumbs like a geriatric pigeon.

I exchanged a look with Dom, and he knew right away what needed doing, giving me a stoic nod.

The gangly, hunched over frame of our grandpa materialized through the screen door leading to the kitchen from outside. Dom pressed himself against the wall next to the door and held his breath. I called out like my Mama was still fit as a fiddle. "Yeah. In here, Grandpa. And no touchin' the stuffing!"

"Aw hell, Kelita. You ain't mellowed out none now you's a college girl. Why don't you lighten up a little for your ol' Grampy."

Grampy? I ain't never called him that in my life. And he never referred to himself that way far back as I can ever recall. I wide-eyed a look at Dom, who just shrugged. No answers there.

Grandpa Dean opened the door, took a few wobbly steps inside and almost slipped on Mama's head before he actually saw the thing.

"Jesus H. Christ on a—"

Dom swung his ax around from his far hand, his right hand, smack dab into Grandpa's chest. It knocked him on his ass and made him wheeze like a dying dog. Blood popped and oozed from his sucking wound, spilling all over his shrunken frame. His John Deere ball cap rolled over to Dom's feet and flopped to its side.

Grandpa Dean, however, was still alive and kicking. He stared a deathly violent hole into me; his judgmental, cataract-laden eyes fixed on mine.

"I knew college was gonna change you two. 'Specially you. Goddam jezebel. Corruptin' his head. You ain't getting' away with—"

Before he could finish his rerun of a tirade, Dom simply stomped on his head with his massive steel-toed boot and crushed it like a hard-boiled ostrich egg. The CRUNCH of his skull absolutely made me puke this time. There went my fuckin' Denver omelet, all over Mama's favorite Moroccan rug. I wasn't ready for that kinda impulsive move. Fuckin' Dom and his surprises.

"What the fuck? We're supposed to do it the right way! Stakes. Beheading. This shit here don't clean up right, not one bit. I ain't doing it, Dom"

"Kel, I ain't seen no fangs on him. Ain't seen 'em on Mama neither. You sure they's vampires?"

"We gotta make 'em show 'em. Like in anger or something, you know? Sorta like brandishing a gun. We caught 'em by surprise, we did. They ain't had time to bare nothin', least of all fangs."

Dom was just a tad bit slow on the uptake. He wasn't stupid or nothing, just unsure of himself. I guess that's why we ended up so close. I'm his confidence and he's my strength.

The blood from Mama's neck stump had reached my Doc Martens. Fuckin' bitch couldn't leave me alone even in death. I scraped my shoes on that shitty Moroccan rug and spat. It was a fake anyhow.

"Go get them stakes 'fore any more kin show up."

Dom gave a reluctant stare for a second then hustled outside to his truck. *Our* truck. We managed to scrape together some cash from odd jobs at school to pay for the finest shitbox this side of the Rockies. It got us from point A to point B and that's all either one of us really gave a hoot about.

My mind sprinted to the inevitable. Who was left now? Cousin Del and his girl Rosario, a pair of fuckass hipsters if there ever was any. Auntie Maybelle and Uncle Jimmy, degenerate gamblers times a billion. Gramma Hilda, she was okay I guess. And little Reby, Uncle Frank's youngest. Can't believe they turned *Reby*. She's only five. Or was she six? I mean, was there no shame? No rules to this vampire hoo-ha? Maybe they just ate her outright. Fuckin' hell. Be easier than looking after a five-year-old vampire, I know that.

And then there was Daddy. We hadn't really accounted for him at all yet. Mama told us he was at the store. But that wasn't under duress or nothing, know what I mean? We didn't have time for that before it all went to donkey shit. Her nitpicking our faults all to Hell. Or what she saw as our faults. Mocking our reliance on each other. Saying we were sick in the head. The nerve of her and her fuckin' high horse. Even when staring down certain impalement and a beheading, she was cuntily defiant to the very fuckin' end. I looked at her disembodied head. The blood was congealing with her bullshit perm. I could hear Dom slammin' the door to the truck just outside. He'd be here in a second. And then we'd have to talk about how to deal with Daddy.

I didn't *want* to kill our father. Of all our family, he was the one who sympathized with us the most. Besides Uncle Tolliver, of course. Daddy would regale us with stories of when he was in the Army and was stationed in Italy, South Korea, Germany, and Japan. All the adventures he would have with his buddies. Weird anecdotes about life in the hurry-up-and-wait era of the military. When there were no wars to fight. When it was just about a job and working toward the weekend in a far-off land. I loved those stories. Dom loved them, too. Made me want to get out there and put life in a headlock. Take it for my very own. He wanted us to go to college, but he was married to Mama, and she was the pants of the family. The pants, the shirt, the shoes. The whole fuckin' outfit. He had about as much say as Mr. Crinkly, our ancient bloodhound. That dog seemed to live forever. Maybe they turned him, too? Fuckin' bloodsuckin' vultures.

"Here."

Dom was back with a passel of stakes. More than both of us could equip and still be effective at killing.

"Where we supposed to put 'em all? I said a few. Not the whole fuckin' tree."

"You just said stakes. No mention of how many, even in a general sense."

"You sassin' me?"

"What are we gonna do about Daddy?"

As usual, Dom cut to the chase. No banter in this here dojo.

"You heard Mama. Said he was at the store. Could be true. Dark out. Plausible. But she coulda been coverin' for him. Maybe he's out suckin' the blood from Mr. Dixon's horses over yonder. Maybe even turnin' girls as young as Reby."

"Daddy would nev—"

"I know. But he ain't daddy no more. He's a servant of Lucifer now. Just like Mama. Just like Grandpa Dean."

"I mean, I guess, but—"

"You ever call him Grampy before? Ever?" I nodded at Grandpa. Flies were already all over his head smear. Dom went quiet for a moment. Searchin' through his memory banks for any instance of that name, most likely.

"No. I mean, I don't think so, Kel. If I did, it was when I was real little like. When *we* were real little. You know?"

"You don't *think* so? Maybe that's somethin' you should have told me before you killed him."

"I shrugged 'cause that was my answer. I don't know. I'm not sure. It sounded kinda familiar, but I just don't know for sure. Don't know how else to say it to you. He's dead. Mama's dead. We need to clean them up before—"

"Before what? Before your dear old Daddy arrives?"

And there he was. Still slim and snaky, still wearing loose-fitting clothes he procured from Goodwill. His wild sprout of soil-brown hair directly on top of his noggin looked just the same as when we'd left. He must've slipped in through the side entrance to the kitchen. The one that led to the rest of the downstairs. Didn't even hear him come in. Or he'd always been here. Watching. Either way, it was total vampire bullshit. Had to be. No other way round it.

"Daddy…?"

I thought I was going to be strong when I saw him, but my voice betrayed my proto-adulthood and sent me all the way back to when I was eight years old, and Daddy was the only person in the world to me.

"Hey, Kel. Missed you. Dom. Ya look good. Sorry I couldn't be there for your last tournament. Been busy around here."

No smile. No mischievous mirth in his voice like in better days. Just an air of supreme disappointment. Didn't seem too broken up about Mama, though.

"I bet."

My acidic sarcasm was back. And in good time. There was no turning back from what had to be done now. No matter what happened next, it was going to fuck me up for the rest of my life.

"Now hold on. I see what's going on here. I know you and your mother ain't seen eye-to-eye for, well, maybe forever. And Dean here probably enabled her behavior toward the two of you. I get that. And you know I sympathize. But it's got to stop right here and now."

"Daddy, she said we gotta kill everyone. You's cursed and that's that. I ain't done wrong by her and she ain't by me, neither.

"What time is everyone else comin' over? Tell us and we'll make it easy on you."

Daddy just stared at me. He usually gesticulated every verbal thought with wild yet smooth hand gestures. But this time he just dropped his arms to his side and shook his head.

"What did we do wrong? What did *I* do?"

"When the fuck are they comin'?!"

I was lettin' rage and impatience guide me now, ignoring my ties to my father completely.

"Kel, honey, just calm down and we can talk about this. If you just go, I can clean this up. I won't tell no one. Not a soul. You have my word. You can just skedaddle on back to college like this never even happened."

Dom took a step forward to Daddy, like he wanted to hug him. He almost dropped his stake in the process, the careless oaf.

"Godammit, Dom. Stay the fuck where you are. You think he's just gonna come out and say he's a vampire? Think for a second! Christ almighty."

Daddy did a double take and flinched. He was a great fucking actor. Being an agent of Satan probably helped with the deception.

"What in the Lord's name are you on about, Kel? Dom, what has she been tellin' you? Is this from some elective you kids are taking?"

Dom shot me a pitiful glance. I knew what it meant. I meant to give him a nod back, but I just started hollerin' at Daddy full bore.

"We know what y'all are. We been knowing about it for a time now. Y'all think we're stupid. That we're just a couple of dumbass kids looking to escape the farm. That was the plan at first, yeah. Then y'all started changing. Didn't take us long to figure out what exactly into."

Daddy took a few steps closer to me. I gotta admit, I almost caved like Dom. But one of us had to be the strong one. Usually, it was him. Not this time.

"Stay the fuck back!"

"Just tell me where you got this damn fool idea. You can tell me. It's okay."

He reached out a hand to me and I wanted to take it so very badly. This must be what it feels like when the Devil jumps up and tempts you with that thing you want more than anything else in this world. I slapped his arm away and backed up 'bout as many steps as he had advanced.

"Spaghetti dinners!" I shouted with wounded rage. There. He couldn't deny *that* shit.

"What?"

"Uncle Frank's spaghetti dinners. Stopped when he died. Why? Maybe because there's garlic in spaghetti! You think we wouldn't notice?"

"Jesus Christ. Kiddo, you got the wrong idea. Mama adored your Uncle Frank. She didn't want anything reminding her of him like that anymore. It was just too much for her. And when she makes up her mind, you know how that goes."

"Oh yeah? What about how you sucked Uncle Frank dry like the vampire fucks that you are?"

"You were at the funeral. We buried Uncle Frank."

"The funeral we had at night? Who the fuck does that? And what about what I found out back behind the barn? Uncle Frank's work clothes? The one's he had on when he keeled over? Where's your excuse for *that*?"

I could see Dom shiftin' in his boots, not knowing who to believe. Frankly, it pissed me off, after all we'd been through. All the plotting, planning. Reassuring ourselves that this was the right way to handle things. Who the fuck did he think he was?

"Hold tight, Dom," I said to my brother, trying to shake out the shake in my voice. I wasn't going to let him fall apart now.

"You know he's lying. That's why he didn't go to your matches at the tournament. Daylight. They can't go out in that shit no more. We been over this."

"I ain't what you say, kiddos. It's just me. Always been me. This family had a hard time coping with your uncle's passing. He was the center of everything. That don't heal right, not even over a bushel of time."

"The late nights? The partyin'? Bringin' strange people home and never seein' them again? That part of the coping process?"

I was just about through with the explanations. It was time to move straight to the conclusion of this here fool's parade.

"Yeah, I'll admit we were off our kilter. Late nights drinking and gambling. We were still grieving, and it was the summer. You kids were off school. We thought you could handle some freedom for a while. We got carried away, we know. But that ain't no reason to think we're vampires. Thought you were above crazy conspiracy theories, Kel. That what they're teaching you in college?"

"I wanna believe you, Daddy; I really do, but there ain't no turning back for us—"

Something faint caught my ear through the long, dark distance of the East Texas flatlands.

Were those sirens?

"The fuck is that? You call the fuckin' cops?"

Dom started a low-key panic mid-sentence. "D-dad? You said we could leave. You said you'd take care of this—"

"I know what I said, boy. And I meant it. You had your window to leave. And your sister, stubborn as she is, didn't take it. Now we all gotta face the truth. This is for your protection as much as it is for your own good. She's turning you sour, Dom. Can't you see it?"

He reached out for Dom and went to embrace him. And that was it. I could picture Daddy ripping out Dom's neck with his fangs and I just lost it. With an inhuman scream, I charged at Daddy and stabbed him in the back with a fresh stake. The shocked scream he let out almost stayed my attack permanently. It reminded me of when our other Grandpa, Papa Sam, Daddy's daddy, died. It was the only other time I ever seen Daddy so racked with grief and pain.

"Dom…" Daddy managed to gurgle out my brother's name with rigid agony.

"Now, Dom, finish him! Don't let him bite you!"

Whether it was out of fear of me, or he was picturin' the same fate for him as I had just seen in my own mind's eye, Dom slashed his ax down the face and chest of Daddy with a panicked swipe. It sliced a huge swath of upturned, bloody flesh. Dom's ax blade went right through Daddy's stomach even quicker than butter that had been sittin' out all night on the kitchen counter next to the stove. Our father's intestines flopped onto the floor in a steamy pile of viscera with a damp, muffled series of smacks that threatened to trigger my vomit reflex one more time.

It looked like to me that he almost shook his head in disapproval. Like he planned on Dom turnin' on me and rightin' all of this. And he would get Mama dead in the deal. And Dean. He always hated Dean. Dom as a vampire palling it up with Daddy made my stomach turn over and over and over.

"Fucking kill him! Now!" I was almost taken aback at how much I sounded like my mother in that moment. The tone. The voice. The pitch. Everything.

I didn't have to yell again 'cause Dom impaled our dad through the heart with the hilt end of his ax, pulled it back out with a sick suctioning sound, gripped the bloody handle, and chopped off his head. It only took two hard, powerful whacks. On the first hit, Daddy's eyes almost popped out. The second hit sent his head rolling over close by to Mama's head. Together in death. Fuck 'em. That's what he gets for staying with her.

Dom was breathing hard and heavy. We looked into each other's eyes and fell back into sync. It was time to prepare for the rest of the family's arrival. I pictured cleaving Reby in two with Dom's ax and it excited and frightened me all at once. That is, if she hadn't already been eaten by her own kin. I bet Grandpa Dean would have been the culprit. Fuckin' handsy old creep.

The sirens were much closer now. An indifferent, unavoidable march of fate and random force. Coming straight for us. No time to make a proper break for it now. They *had* to be in on it. Fuckin' bloodsuckin' pigs.

It was nice to know we had more than enough stakes for the occasion, though. Just a truck's bed away.

I gave Dom a reassuring smile. He deserved at least that after what we just been through.

"Cops'll be here any second," Dom droned as he readied his ax.

"Good. And make sure you make 'em show their fuckin' fangs this time."

NOTES

This was originally published in early 2021 in the anthology *Family* from Terror Tract Publishing. Terror Tract folded unceremoniously in 2022, and I felt that this story deserved better. For what it's worth, this might be the most fun I've had with a short story up to this point. That's why I wanted it to be the first one up to bat in this collection. It all goes back to spaghetti dinners in real life for me. My family on my dad's side all moved from

Massachusetts to retire to the Chesapeake area in Virginia. My grandparents and a host of great aunts and uncles and a few cousins. One great uncle in particular, my Uncle Bert, loved hosting spaghetti dinners with tons of family in attendance as a prelude to the most foul-mouthed all-night game of poker you would ever be allowed to witness as a kid. After a while, everyone got older and started dying off. Uncle Bert didn't feel like doing spaghetti dinners much anymore. I wanted to write a story where the deep grief of a family death radically alters the family dynamic itself forever. When someone in your tribe dies, it forever changes the way that tribe interacts for good. I've never had any issues with either side of my family and hanging out with them or gathering with them for special occasions. We're not all perfect, but we enjoy each other's company unironically. As I get older, I recognize that's not the case with a lot of people. I consider myself lucky I had a fun, funny, and mostly supportive extended family. That old specter of death looms larger and larger with every family function. One more funeral to dread. One less wedding to look forward to. Soon, all you're left with are a bunch of funerals and no more weddings. It sucks and even if you're not on the best terms with your family, I still think a little piece of you dies with them every time. For better or for worse. Even if you don't feel it until much later in your life. Well, that was a bummer explanation of a fun, fucked up story. Sorry!

WELCOME TO THE SHOW

The first time Bret mentioned something about a secret sex show somewhere on the island, Steph balked and changed the subject. Something about what was for dinner later that night.

The second time he shoehorned it into conversation, she nodded and listened with faux intent. Hoped he would trail off eventually and be done with it.

The third time, it caused an argument between them so fierce, that Pat and Mel left the suite to go drink elsewhere.

The four of them had already been in Cozumel for half of their ten-day vacation and it felt every minute of it and then some to Steph. She'd never admit that to Bret, but she knew this talk of the fabled exhibition was a result of beach fatigue and sexual frustration.

From their home in Des Moines, a week-and-a-half on the sand drinking and tanning sounded like the daily regimen of gods and royalty. Now it seemed like a prelude to the ennui of middle-agedness.

The bed sheets were cool, and the room was silent, both enveloping her in complete indifference. Patrick and Melinda still hadn't returned from wherever they scurried off to. Bret was still out after their blowup. Although she felt justified in starting it, she did feel a pang of remorse for some of the things she said to him. Calling him a pervert sent a shock of surprise right to his face that she'd never seen before. It unnerved her. She was apparently capable of hurting someone she'd never seen shed one single tear for anything.

Not being able to sleep shifted from her main concern to number two or three as the thought of Bret's motives behind wanting her to go to such a show ballooned into a full-blown mental investigation. Esteban was the name of the bellboy that told him about the place. At least, that's what Bret claimed. Punta Vista. Not on any map. Only known to locals. Dive bars, strip clubs, makeshift casinos. Drinks and drugs; buffet-style. It all sounded like some kind of trap for foreigners to lose all their money to the federales or even the cartel.

That should have been it, but something nagged at the back of her brain. Something vague about escaping the boredom of their all-inclusive resort. Comfortably suffocating. Listening to kids squawk at the breakfast buffet for no good reason. Being within earshot of old people complaining about anything and everything so they don't keel over and die for lack of purpose. Forced to witness other couples arguing about politics or religion or whatever regurgitated talking points floated into their bird brains. She felt comfortable among these simpletons once. Unchallenging, non-threatening simpletons. Marching toward the cliff of inevitable mortality. It wasn't until they met Mel and Pat on a trip to San Francisco a few years ago that she started to see underneath the façade of the endless parade of judgmental, consumerist morons that parade about like penguins on an iceberg.

Simply put, Mel was a masochist and Pat was a sadist and they couldn't get enough of each other. At first, their alarming chemistry put Steph off from the word "go." Bret warmed to them right away, however. He saw them as harmless party animals. Mel drank too much, and Pat thirsted for anything happening on the wild side of night life anywhere they went. When Steph had bluntly asked Bret if going to the exhibition was Pat's idea, Bret visibly sulked into himself. Offended that she saw him as an empty-headed follower. His words, not hers. He insisted it was his idea and that he hadn't even told Pat yet.

She was the first to know.

Thinking back, she realized what he was trying to do. Her repeated denials of the idea were just her being annoyed at herself for not seizing the moment. Such a thing takes more effort than you would think. Seizing anything seemed exhausting after succumbing to everyday married life.

A lukewarm breeze pushed its way through the curtains leading to their balcony. It was a beautiful suite; two huge bedrooms, one for each couple, and a massive living area all decorated Roman Empire-style and colored in pleasing Mediterranean faded pastels.

As luxurious as it was, nothing truly exciting happened in there. Mel and Pat engaged in loud, obnoxious drunken balling that never lasted long or even finished. Bret had tried to initiate a few times since they arrived, and she pretended to be asleep or just politely declined. She just hadn't felt like it and didn't have the drive to tell him it wasn't his fault. Lately she hadn't been up for much of anything and even considered cancelling the trip altogether, though Bret put his foot down and insisted they go for the health of their relationship. Something about bringing them closer together.

Why he thought she would say yes to checking out a sex show was eluding her. Was that a good or bad thing? How did he see her now? After all they had been through, was this what it all came down to? Watching some girl shoot ping pong balls out of her vagina or a dirty older couple copulate under hot lights? To witness *that* as a couple? What would it do for their relationship? What did he know that she didn't?

Usually on vacations, couples end up fucking more and not less. So far, this general truth had eluded her and Bret. Maybe this is what he'd been hinting at all along. His way of trying to spice things up. It made her laugh, and her laugh sounded bizarre in that darkened, otherwise empty suite.

The sounds of the beach just outside of their suite soon overtook the remnants of her laugh and left her with nothing.

Except Esteban.

That was definitely the bellboy's name.

* * *

The front desk was aglow with a myriad of lights coming from the floor, the ceiling, from every which way but sideways. The concierge was a trim and fit fortysomething Mexican man with the neatest, cleanest mustache Steph had ever seen. He was dressing down a young bellboy wearing a wrinkled uniform and a crooked nametag. As Steph neared, she squinted to see his name on said tag.

Miguel.

Doesn't even rhyme with Esteban.

She waited statue-still for the concierge to finish his riot act in Spanish. Miguel barely flinched, like he'd been here before. Several times before. After a few more moments, Miguel shuffled off at the dismissive signal from the concierge's gloved hands. Steph cleared her throat and waited for the concierge to notice her. He spun around at her throat noises and forced a polite, toothy smile of service.

"Yes, how may I help you, my dear?"

"Um, yes, I'm looking for Esteban. He's a bellboy here, I think."

"Is there a problem with your room or our service? Did he—"

"Oh no, no not at all. I just need to uh, I need to talk to him. Is he working?"

The concierge hid his teeth but kept the smile.

"I'm sorry, I cannot give out such information. I can relay a message to him if you'd like."

18

"Oh no, thank you. Never mind. I'm sure I'll see him around. Thanks again."

He nodded once and closed his eyes as he spoke with the same smile.

"But of course. I am at your service if you need anything else, my dear."

She remembered which way Miguel made off and casually followed the trail down the hall to an exit that led outside to a large patio with tables and chairs still available for use. The small bar there was closed, however. She could hear the sounds of the one open nightclub in the distance. People having fun. Probably no one there looking for a hidden ping pong pussy ball show.

Miguel was propped up against a wall, smoking a cigarette and quietly laughing to himself.

"Good joke?" Steph reached for his cigarette, and he obliged, allowing her to take a drag.

"It's more of a local thing, gringas wouldn't understand. Sorry."

She handed the cigarette back to him and tried to act cool, like they were in a movie filled with witty characters that always say the right thing.

"Try me."

"No."

And that was the end of that.

"Do you know Esteban?"

That made Miguel laugh even harder.

"What's funny this time?"

"Yeah, I do."

"And...?"

"And what, chica?"

"Is he around right now?"

"Yeah, he's probably selling drugs to gringas like you over by the pool. Or maybe the nightclub. One of those two for sure."

"That was easy. Thought I was gonna have to bribe you or something."

"I'll take twenty bucks, so no one tells management you were trying to buy drugs off us."

Well played. She didn't even argue. Just pulled out a wad of cash from her jeans pocket. Peeled off a twenty and dangled it in front of Miguel.

"Is there really a secret sex club out there somewhere?"

Miguel waited a long moment before he unleashed a knowing grin.

"Do you want the answer to be yes or no?"

The question gave Steph pause. What did she want the answer to be?

"The pool or the club, huh?"

Miguel's face curled upwards, appreciating her directness.

"The club."

Steph handed him the twenty and left with a matching smirk.

* * *

Morning came. So did poolside for breakfast. Steph found herself seated opposite three extremely hungover individuals. Complete with sunglasses to hide their beyond bloodshot eyes and assorted hats to block out the interloping, rising sun.

"That's all it took? Twenty bucks?" Bret was waiting for the punchline to come. His patchwork beard seemed to bristle with excitement at the news Steph brought.

"Plus the hundred I gave to Esteban." Steph's proud smile crumpled a bit as she admitted to parting ways with a Ben Franklin.

"A-ha. I knew there was a catch." Patrick never met an inconvenient time to be an asshole.

"What he means to say is thank you, Steph." Mel was trying to support her, but Steph knew she was just putting on a front. She was as pushy as Pat when it came to dominating a conversation.

Bret was now speechless. This was what he wanted all along, but he seemed hesitant still.

"Esteban said he'll pick us up out front at six tonight. Sharp. If we're not there right at six, we're out of luck."

"You two are best buds now, huh? What else did it take to get him to drive us there?" Patrick legitimately wanted to know, and it seemed to bother him no one else thought of this idea before he did.

"Back to tonight's entertainment. Cool?" Steph was getting comfortable steering things her way for a change. She could see why Patrick did it so much.

"What's the one thing?" Bret leaned into her like she was telling him his fortune or something.

"Well, a few things. One. When we get there, we'll have a while before the club opens up at midnight. We have to do the whole bar crawl all the way to the place and give them the password at midnight. No earlier. No later."

"What's the password? Is it "I love chimichangas?"" Patrick was proud of that one but even Mel didn't laugh. Steph was mildly impressed at her restraint.

"Nah, it's probably something like 'Do you want us to take you to America?'" Mel sounded out America like she was explaining the word to a child with a head injury. Steph's mild admiration for Mel disappeared faster than a Long Island Iced Tea did down Mel's throat.

"The password is *placer*."

"Is that French?" Bret was trying his best to be supportive in his own way.

"It's the Spanish word for pleasure."

"Where's the fucking waitress? I'm hungrier than a hostage over here." Patrick was visibly unimpressed with anything Steph had conveyed so far.

"What do you want, babe? I'll go get it for you." Mel the gopher. In the flesh.

"Guys. Please. She's trying to tell us how to get there. This is what we've been talking about for days now. It's finally happening!" Bret the peacemaker. Steph was starting to warm up to him now. After all, wasn't she doing this for him? At least that's what she told herself last night in the empty hotel suite with nothing but the tide to confide in.

"Pleasure, huh?" Mel put a hand on Patrick's thigh, soothing the horny beast for now. "I like it."

"It's fitting, I think." Bret put an arm around Steph, satisfied his bugaboo for this vacation was alive and well thanks to his wife. Steph cozied up to him, forcing herself to be in the moment.

"Anything else, detective?" Pat was as flippant as ever, but in a much more hushed, relaxed tone thanks to Mel's thigh massage.

"First sign of danger, real danger, we're outta there. For real. That's my condition for agreeing to all this."

Pat rolled his eyes while Mel just stared at her.

"That seems fair." Bret knew where his bread was buttered and squeezed Steph tight in his arms.

"I'm not kidding. If there's so much as a bar fight, we're done. We're there for this show you can't stop talking about and that's it.

"Okay, that's it." Bret nodded, but a little too much.

"You guys are so fucking boring. This place is gonna be lame. Bunch of strippers in pasties kissing each other while the DJ jerks off in the corner. Real fucking exciting." Patrick made any event sound like it could give you a solid case of hepatitis.

"Just wait, I've heard this place will change your life. For the better." Bret gazed into Steph's eyes and for a second she returned his love with an equal amount of gaze until she realized what she had gotten herself into.

Bret and Steph kissed a kiss of desperate hope as Patrick yelled for a server while Mel rubbed his shoulders, purring like a kitten all the while.

"I hope so."

Steph stared into the middle distance, hoping to see anything but the concierge staring at her from the patio across the way. A flicker of a smile flashed for just a second.

*   *   *

The suite was almost as quiet as last night. Mel and Pat were napping off the last chunk of their brutal hangovers. The occasional snore was the only thing that emanated from their room.

Steph and Bret stretched out on their bed, semi-entwined in each other. Pensive looks on their faces. For two people supposedly going out to paint the town red, as it were, they looked like they were on their way to the funeral of a loved one. Not too loved, but loved nonetheless.

Bret brushed away a lock of her cinnamon hair from her face. "You sure about this? I mean, for real."

"Yeah. I mean, I thought about it long and hard after…"

"I know. I'm sorry for pushing. I just…"

"It's okay, I promise. After talking to Esteban, I feel better. I swear I had it in my mind you were trying to take us to some kind of orgy or something."

"Oh no, babe. I would nev—"

"I know, I know. It's just—"

"Exhibition shows have a long tradition going back to ancient times. They're just not that widely accepted anymore. Especially in a country like this. I can't wait to share this experience with you."

"Exhibition? Sex show. Just say it."

"Will that make you happier?"

"A little. In this moment."

"Okay."

Bret kissed Steph quietly, smoothly. A boyish smile plastered on his kissing lips.

"Sex…"

Steph was aroused for the first time since they arrived in Cozumel. She pushed her body in closer to Bret and kissed him back.

"…Show." Bret whispered in between kisses.

This had to be a good sign for the night ahead. They would be on the same page for the first time since being on vacation.

As Bret slid a hand down her jeans, she felt something for tonight that she hadn't felt in a very long time.

Excitement.

* * *

The sun was still going strong as Steph, Bret, Pat, and Mel approached the muddy red Jeep parked in the roundabout in front of the resort's front entrance. It looked as out of place as Pat and Mel did at any establishment with a dress code.

Esteban was talking to Miguel in Spanish, occasionally trading deep belly laughs between each other, looking around every now and then.

"I hate that shit. Speak English. Probably talking about us. Bet you a hundred bucks." Pat grinned at Steph, thinking that was a savage callback.

"Why would they be speaking English? We're in their country, for fuck's sake." Steph was roughly two more shitty comments away from kicking him in the dick.

"Relax, he's just kidding. Jesus." Mel fell all over herself again to prove she was loyal to her man.

"We get it, you don't have to defend him every time."

Mel stared bug-eyed at Steph, unsure of how to come back from such a simple, yet hard truth.

"Well, with these resorts, it's kind of like foreign soil. You know what I mean? English probably just puts the tourists at ease." Steph knew Bret was trying to play peacemaker, but even that line of logic was too much for him to really believe. It probably hurt coming out, but he most likely sensed a fight brewing between his wife and his friend and wanted to end it before it was past the point of no return.

Honorable but still shitty.

Esteban whispered something into Miguel's ear before heading over to the four, clapped his hands and rubbed them together with unbridled vigor. "You ready for a crazy ass night?"

Steph shot a nod at Miguel, hoping to get one back. None came. He just looked her up and down before returning inside.

It bothered her, but not enough to throw her off her high. She and Bret had finally fucked for the first time since being in Mexico and her legs still thrummed from the solid orgasm his tongue had delivered. It was so satisfying that she immediately blew him afterwards. And that was something she did rarely; it almost sent Bret tumbling over the bed and onto the floor in shock.

"Look, I'm not gonna lie, I'm kinda calling bullshit on this sex place." Pat's braying mouth snapped Steph back to reality.

"Oh yeah?" Esteban looked like he was about to giggle at the gringo's adorable posturing.

"Yeah. How fucking wild can it really be?"

"It's not on the map for a reason, jefe."

"Good point. He's got you there, man." Bret elbowed his way into the exchange, adding absolutely nothing.

"Are we going or not?" Mel sighed, already tired of all the talky talk.

Esteban leaned an elbow on Steph. "She tell you what I told her yet?"

"Yeah, yeah. Let's go already." Patrick was dangerously close to dick kicking territory.

"One more thing." Esteban dropped the jokey demeanor and got dead serious.

Patrick looked like he was about to have a temper tantrum right there at the entrance to the Playa Vista International Resort. "Jesus Meximelting Christ, what is it?"

"Have fun!" Esteban threw some mock punches in the vicinity of Pat and Bret, playfully dancing around them like a sprightly boxer.

"We plan on it," Steph smiled coyly at Bret.

Esteban hopped into the driver's seat of the Jeep and whistled. "All aboard! Choo-choo!"

Pat pushed his way to the passenger's seat. "Shotgun!"

Steph feigned applause for him. "No one cares."

"That's what losers say!"

The other three piled into the back of the Jeep and braced themselves as Esteban peeled out and sped off down the main road leading away from the resort. Away from civilization, maybe? Steph couldn't help but think that. There was no backing out now. She'd never hear the end of it.

From Mel. From Pat.

From Bret.

*　*　*

The ride to Punta Vista wasn't even an hour. A breezy sprint through bumpy backroads, passing the occasional shack or hut. This was clearly the small section of the island the tour buses and taxis stayed away from. The townie area, as Bret would say.

The closer they got to their destination, the more Steph felt like she was intruding. No matter how much fun Esteban said they would have or how it was okay for them to be there.

Intruders. One and all.

Every now and then, she'd catch the eyes of a local whizzing by, and they weren't the eyes of someone happy to see a tourist right outside their home. *Stay the fuck on the resort*, those eyes said.

"This is it! You guys ready for this shit?" Esteban's voice insisted sincerity, but it felt even more tacked on than normal. It didn't sit well in the pit of Steph's stomach.

"Fuck yeah, man." Pat bro-elbowed Esteban, a sign of his begrudging approval. Esteban didn't even flinch or smile. A dad dropping off the kids at school who couldn't wait to get rid of them so he could go home and fuck the maid.

As the Jeep slowed to an amble and moved through the gates to Punta Vista, they were all regaled with the craziest looking shanty town anyone could ever have imagined. Like a port of call from a pirate gangster movie where everything looked like it was coated in old cocaine. Thumping house music from strobed-up clubs clashed with drunken mariachi bands stumbling throughout the streets, busking for puke-encrusted dollar bills. Tourists from all over the world, it seemed, snaked to-and-fro from establishment to establishment, drunk or high or both. Clothes peeled off here or there, strangers making out with other strangers.

"God damn. You weren't lying, ese!" Patrick hopped out of the Jeep and marveled at his surroundings for the next five hours plus.

Bret had only one thing on his mind. "Where is it?"

"Relax, man." Esteban cooed at Bret and pointed to the end of the strip. "You see it?"

All the way down, past all the horny hullabaloo, was a small, shitty bar with a busted blue neon sign.

It read "**BAR AVALON**."

A lofty claim for such a dive.

"That's it?" Mel spoke for everyone else with her unimpressed query.

"Uh, are you sure, sir?" Bret insisted on manners even in a place like this. It was kind of cute.

"Yeah, dude. What's wrong? I know she don't look like much on the outside, but on the inside is where you'll bust your load."

Bret ventured an appalled look across his face, kneejerk quick. "It's not like that—"

"Whatever, man. Go have fun. Just don't fuck with the cartel."

"What?" Mel almost dropped her clutch in the mud.

"Kidding, kidding. But seriously, there are federales here. And they love money and fucking with Americans. Don't let your dicks hang out too far. Half these idiots walking around are gonna have empty wallets and splitting headaches when the sun comes back around."

"Thanks for the tip, bro." And with that, Pat sauntered off to mingle with his people. Mel trotted after him, shouting something about "other pussy."

Bret motioned for Steph to head out, but something was nagging at her. It grew and grew on the ride here and now it had to be itched.

"Are you sure we're safe here?"

Esteban dropped down from the driver's seat and leaned on the Jeep uncomfortably close to her.

"You ever been to Bourbon Street?"

"Sure."

"Tijuana?"

"Once."

"How about Bangkok?"

"I have. A while ago, I mean." Bret shrugged at Steph after blurting out this new-to-her info.

"Did your dick fall off? Did you get arrested for carrying dope?"

"No. But I did have really good noodles at this place that looked kinda dangerous. Like, they said triads ate there all the time."

Esteban smirked sideways at Steph and stepped backwards into the driver's seat.

"See? You guys aren't fucking idiots. You'll be fine."

Esteban revved up the Jeep and prepared to peel out.

"Just make sure you're in there at midnight. Don't forget the password. And for the love of God, once you're inside don't talk back to anyone and do exactly what they tell you."

And with that, he made his exit. Not a care of concern for them whatsoever. A teenage cousin convincing his younger relatives to throw rocks at the mentally handicapped kid's house down the street.

* * *

The next five hours dragged like the longest line of blow in the world chased with two dozen boilermakers. From bar-to-bar and club-to-club, Steph, Bret, Pat, and Mel drank, got high, danced, argued, and flirted with anyone and anything in their path.

Throughout this, Bret checked his watch on the half hour without fail. In between that, he insisted on trying to soften up Steph to what was about to happen at midnight. Like she needed convincing. They were already there and on top of that he really had no fucking clue what was behind those ramshackle doors.

Pat and Mel were so blottoed, they tried to hit on each other without realizing they were already together. It took all of Bret's reserved masculine manners to keep Pat from

29

fighting a sorority from Tallahassee over a fifty-dollar bill laying in an alley, already soaked in piss.

And that was only at nine o'clock. Twenty-one hundred hours. Still three to go.

*   *   *

Those last three hours were a litany of slurred pickup lines, projectile vomiting into cleavage, and the worst white person style of dancing known to humankind.

Steph was ready to leave at ten and downright bored at eleven. She was drunk but nowhere near drunk enough to not give a shit about her own wellbeing.

She was sure a fedérale tried to proposition her a little after eleven. She was polite enough but passed him on to Mel. Steph was ninety percent certain Mel blew him in the bathroom of whatever club they were in. The one blasting a Tejano remix of Cotton Eyed Joe. Pat was so into staring at the half-covered ass of a Bolivian girl that had to be no older than sixteen that he had no idea such a thing had even transpired.

At eleven-thirty, Steph had reached her tolerance of booze and shenanigans.

"What time is it?" To his credit, Bret was the only one in their group who still actually wore a watch on his wrist.

"Eleven-thirty." She could tell he was right behind her on the listless boredom train. She could hear it in his shitfaced exhale of a response.

"One last round of fucking shots before we make for the freak show!" Patrick bumped into Steph like he wanted to dance. It only served to annoy her even further.

"Fuck off."

"Oh come on, one more shot! Don't penis out! See, I can be a feminist, too!"

30

She was ready to just sign off on the whole Pat and Mel project for good and she could see even Bret was arriving there as well.

One more shot. For the road. Fuck it.

"Bring it on, cocksucker."

"Stop talking about yourself!"

To anyone else, that might have sounded like a flirtatious exchange, but Bret and Mel knew it was the path to a punch-up. They intervened in kind.

"I'll get them. Be right back!" Mel scooted off to grab four more double shots of tequila.

"I'll help." Bret followed her, screaming a bunch of uselessness and redundancy into the noise of the night. Steph could pinpoint his desperation miles away. She stared a crater into Pat's dry, sunburned scowl.

"What?"

"Don't fuck this up for him."

Instead of an argument, Pat actually backed off. "Aye-aye, cap'n."

Steph was almost disappointed in the lack of confrontation. An anticlimax in a place filled with climaxes of all sorts. She didn't even know what to say next. She just gaped at him until Mel and a trailing Bret returned with four double shots of cheap, shitty tequila. The kind that made your stomach wish it were born as any other organ in your body.

"Here's to a new adventure. May we all be changed from it. For the better." Bret's toast was too subtle and polite for their surroundings.

"Whatever the fuck that means. Bottoms up!" Pat replied.

They downed their shots and looked around the club at the writhing throng of horny college kids and tourists.

"Shit, I'm gonna remember this night forever." Mel stammered her appreciation with barely English words as she crammed all four lemons in her mouth at once.

"Almost midnight." Steph wasn't going to let them forget the task at hand. And the fact that this night was thankfully almost over.

"Thank you, babe. This will bring us together. I promise. And I'm sorry for pushing you into things." She knew he was genuine, but that nagging feeling in the back of her mind made his words seem flaccid and emasculated. Worthless.

Dangerous.

* * *

No one else waited in front of the Bar Avalon at 11:59 PM. Was this a special attraction just for them? An off night for the featured talent? Steph had a shitload of questions and no one to answer them. No doorman, no nothing.

"Are we sure we're at the right place?" It was Mel's attempt to sound caring and somewhat with it, despite her severe inebriation.

"Where the fuck else we gonna wait? We already tore through every other place in this shithole."

"It's midnight." Bret was about to hyperventilate with excitement. Steph wanted to share that titillation with him, but in that moment, being there felt enough. Especially now that she had a crumb of doubt festering in her brain.

No sooner than Bret had announced the local time, a tall and worn-out old Mexican gentleman in faded biker attire appeared through the flung-open front door. He sized up the four of them and folded his arms, joints creaking and cracking with arthritis every which way.

"Which one of you shitheads has the password?"

Patrick almost bowed up to him, but Mel grabbed his arm and gave it a brisk massage. Crisis averted.

"Placer." Steph refused to waste any more time with this bizarre ordeal.

32

Old Man Biker looked at Bret, guessing he was with Steph and chortled. "The women have bigger dicks than the men in whatever shit town you come from?"

Bret just wanted in. "Some do, yeah. I guess."

"Ha! Get the fuck in here. Jesus, man." He waved them on in with a who-gives-a-shit gesture and a painful flourish of his hips.

*　*　*

Inside was even more embarrassing than the exterior. A spacious, poorly lit excuse for a ballroom with about eight or nine large round tables on the dancefloor with a rickety assortment of chairs and stools to accompany them. Some had tablecloths, some didn't.

It looked like the bartender was getting a blowjob from someone underneath the bar, but it was hard to tell for sure.

About half of the tables were occupied. A dirty and fully tattooed group of bikers at one, a handful of emotionless men in patchwork military gear at another. One had what looked like a family of ranchers and farmers. Mom, dad, some kids even.

Some stared at the newcomers, some didn't. There was no record scratch for their arrival. It was simultaneously comforting and alarming to Steph.

The stage had several red lights shining on it, random things covered in sheets here and there and there were two pairs of weird metal hoops bolted to the floor up there, each pair about ten feet apart from each other. What the fuck kind of show were they going to see? Steph's own red light started to flash weakly in her gut.

As if things couldn't get more off-putting, a squat man in a tattered ringmaster's outfit and a crumpled top hat pushed his way from the back room – demarcated by heavy, black wooden beads that clacked loudly in his wake.

33

"Welcome, welcome, welcome, and…welcome! Please sit down. The show is about to begin."

Bret tried to show his gratitude with effusive thanks, but the diminutive host refused. "Please, please, there's no time. We're starting any minute now that you're here. I'll bring you something to drink. On the house!"

They all exchanged bemused and impressed looks as they took their seat.

"You might be onto something here, dude. Service with a fucking smile. Color me shocked as fuck, ya know?" Patrick could barely string together words, but the others got the gist.

"This shit better be worth it. We could be doing that beer pong shit in the other bar. Remember? That group from Boston seemed cool as fuck."

The red lights all focused to a center point on the stage without any announcement.

"Shhhh, it's starting!" Bret went into full attention mode. Idle chatter could fuck off now.

Apparently, the first act was a middle-aged, ashy-haired Latina woman with amputated arms at the elbows resting on said stumps, completely naked. A dwarf in a blue velour tracksuit jogged up to her with a metal bucket and handed her something from it. A ping pong ball? She smiled a thank you at him and proceeded to pop multiple ping pong balls out of her vagina at varying speeds and distances.

There was no music to accompany her, no announcements, no applause. Just the echo-pop of the balls loosed into the air, eventually clicking to the ground somewhere on the floor here and there.

"Want me to grab one for you, bud?" Pat sounded serious and facetious all at once.

Bret didn't even move a muscle at Pat's offer. He was really into this. It had to be some sort of cultural badge of pride. A story to tell other put-upon husbands at barbecues and playdates. The one thing that would make him interesting as he got older.

The tattered ringmaster brought two bottles of unopened tequila to their table, proudly showing them off with his sausage fingers once they were set down.

He whispered to them as the show continued. "Our finest. It has the worm and everything, my friends." His teeth were grey and crooked. It almost made Steph throw up. That and the thought of drinking more tequila.

"No thanks." She winced, caught between flying ping pong balls and more stomach-churning booze.

"Fuck, More for me then." Pat showed no sign of stopping his rampant indulgence. Neither did Mel, who silently gave him a weak, drunken thumbs up.

Bret looked at the bottle, unsure if he should go for it.

"It's part of the experience, my friend. You don't want to miss out, do you?" And with that tidbit, the host slid off to another table, laughing with them about something Steph would never find out about.

That pricked up Bret's ears. He opened one of the bottles and just started drinking it without the aid of a glass.

"Slow down, hun." Steph's internal red light started flashing a little brighter now. This was not like Bret. Something wasn't right.

"Drink up or shut up, bitch." She could hardly believe what he had just said to her.

"Yeah, bitch, drink that shit!" Even Pat was becoming more aggressive than he had ever been with her. What the fuck was going on?

The ping pong woman was nearing the bottom of her bucket but showed no signs of flagging enthusiasm or loss of speed. It actually kind of annoyed Steph. Even this woman was having fun.

Pat and Bret were now just fisting the tequila bottles and downing them with full-throated sips. Steph feared asking the guys anything else. There was only one appeal left.

"Hey, Mel. You wanna step outside for a little bit? Grab some air?" Steph put on her most polite voice without sounding patronizing, hoping Mel would get the message.

Surprisingly, she did.

"Yeah. Sure." Through her alcohol-induced stupor, even Mel knew something fucked was happening. The look of sudden fear in Mel's eyes awakened the butterflies in Steph's stomach. Everything in here was now officially all wrong. Not subjectively, either.

As Mel got up, Pat grabbed her arm in an iron grip and forced her back down to the table.

"Where the fuck are you going, skank? You leaving me? Huh?"

"No, I... I just wanted to get some air with Steph. That's all."

"You two gonna talk about how small our dicks are, huh? Gonna laugh about how we can't fuck you good as you want? That it?"

Pat grabbed Mel around the neck and squeezed as she began to sob and wheeze in frozen terror.

"Well fuck that shit."

Steph went to reach across the table and free Mel from Pat's grip when Bret of all people grabbed her arm and glared at her.

"Mind your own business, cunt. Or you'll get it next."

Steph had never felt scared to be with Bret. Ever.

Until now.

"Bret, what the fuck..."

"I said shut up! You want me to tell you again, you fucking cocktease?"

"C'mon Mel, we gotta get outta here."

The tattered ringmaster was at their table again, like an apparition with shitty teeth.

"I'm afraid the doors are closed until the show has ended. I'm sorry, my friends."

"What?" Steph had gotten free of Bret and loomed over the smaller man.

"But don't worry! The main event is about to start."

"About fucking time!" Patrick bristled with testosterone; it was oozing into his voice.

"Fuck yeah!" Bret shouted with what sounded like pure anger. Or was it excitement?

To Steph's horror, she could see Bret growing a massive erection in his pants. The more aggressive he became, the more it grew.

"What the fuck…" Steph tried to move for the door, but the old biker doorman intercepted her and pushed her back into her seat.

"I'd really stay there if I were you. You'll see morning if you do."

Steph looked to the stage in a panic and saw it was empty. No armless woman. No dwarf. No ping pong balls. No red lights. Just an empty stage with two spotlights shining on the metal hoops in its floor.

Patrick had finally let go of Mel's throat and was rubbing something below the table line. Steph didn't need to see to know what was happening with him.

Then Steph realized something.

The tequila.

"Stop drinking! Stop drinking the tequila, it's…"

"Fuck off, bitch." Pat was completely lost of all tact, even the little he ever had to begin with.

Bret took another swig of it. "There's nothing wrong with it. Tastes like fucking Cuervo."

Steph slapped the bottle out of his hand. It smashed to the floor. No one else even regarded what was going on at their table. There was some muffled conversation here, some laughter there, but none of it seemed directed at them.

And then it happened.

Patrick shouted something loud and unintelligible as he fell to the floor. His voice growing deeper and more guttural with every second.

"Hurrrrrr… Arrrrrrrggghhhhh…"

Just as Patrick hit the floor, Bret grabbed his stomach in agony.

"Ahhhhhh. Fuuuuck—"

He fell out of his seat and landed on his ass, writhing around and moaning.

Steph and Mel looked at each other in slow a motion panic, not knowing what to do.

Patrick then fell silent, giving the girls a much-needed break. But it was short-lived as a deafening animal bray pierced the room from the floor where Pat resided.

Suddenly it all made sense. The massive pit in Steph's stomach moved to her whole body as she turned to Bret's spot on the floor. He had long, furry ears protruding from his shaggy hair and a ropey tail with a tuft of hair at the end had popped out of his pants. As he pawed at his own massive erection through his corduroy slacks, he stared her dead in the eye and screamed, revealing massive buckteeth growing in the front of his mouth. His awful scream turned to another bray as Steph fainted.

*　*　*

Steph woke to a bright spotlight shining right in her face. She could make out Mel's tear-stained face several feet in front of her. They were both close to the floor. On all fours. The metal hoops on the stage now made sense because they were chained to them by shackles cuffing their hands tight.

Mel looked mentally gone. Nobody home. She still had her blouse on, but Steph noticed that her pants were nowhere to be seen. And what was behind Mel was even more alarming. A jackass with a fully erect cock standing attentively, looking down at Mel's exposed bottom half, inching closer and closer with horny huffs and snuffs through his damp snout.

Steph then noticed a breeze where her own pants should have been. And right after that, she sensed something behind her too. A clicking of big, thick teeth. A clopping of hooves. Inches behind her.

The tattered ringmaster was back. He hopped up on stage and looked to the crowd. It was now a full house. What time was it? Steph's bleary eyes followed him to the table they all once sat around. In their place were four boys, college aged. They hooted and hollered as they went from checking out her and Mel's exposed flesh to laughing at the massive erections of the donkeys behind each girl.

"Gentlemen, ladies, families of all ages, the Bar Avalon humbly welcomes you to our show!"

As Bret's hot breath hit the back of Steph's neck, all she could think of was how he was so insistent on how this trip would bring them closer together.

She wondered if this was close enough for him.

NOTES

This was originally written to submit to *Worst Laid Plans: An Anthology of Vacation Horror*, a book edited and curated by my good friend Samantha Kolesnik and released by the fantastic Grindhouse Press. She didn't feel it was a good fit for the anthology and I think she was right. It was a little too long for their requirements and it takes a while to get going. That's by design, though. I could have put some weirdo stuff in there early on, but I didn't want to show my hand too soon. I feel like the ending more than makes up for it. Did you have a rapier version of Pincocchio on your bingo card? Me neither. This was one of those stories where I just kept pantsing it until the end

and then went back to fine tune the thing. I also didn't want
to make the Mexican locals seem like superstitious adult-
baby caricatures like in a bad horror movie; instead, they
are fully aware of the power they wield and use it to
torment these shitty tourists who don't really give a rat's
ass about their home in the long run. I'd do the same thing.
Not for nothing, but I ended up producing the feature film
adaptation of *Worst Laid Plans* along with Samantha and
it turned out rather awesome, if I do say so myself. If you're
reading this right now, chances are it's playing at a film
festival near you, or it will soon be available on streaming
and disc. There's a lesson here for some of my fellow
writers. My friendship with Samantha is stronger than a
story rejection or some difference of opinion that means
nothing in the grand scheme of things. Getting all huffy
because you didn't get into an anthology and potentially
burn a bridge with someone who's honest with you and
your work would be a stupid thing to do. Also, Samantha's
integrity is beyond reproach. How many other friends
would have just waved me in? I want to get by the right
way, not the friend way. Now go watch *Worst Laid Plans*.
And you're welcome.

FOR MY NEXT SWITCH, I'LL NEED A VOLUNTEER...

My name is Banzo. I know this because the woman screaming at me through the door to my dressing room says so; and I'm the only one in here.

The only *living* being left in here. Banzo the Blinking Clown.

The corpse I gingerly placed in the closet behind me was also named Banzo. He stank of licorice-tinged alcohol and a life of perpetual disappointment; easily mistaken for cigars.

It would be trivial to usurp his achievements but the Creators frown on such things. They want us to exist seamlessly.

Seamlessly.

They're not the ones dropped into these scenarios. Endlessly disposing of bodies, attempting to act natural. Whatever natural signifies today.

"Show's on in five! Get your ass out here now!"

The husky woman's voice slams past the sanctity of my locked door and infects my chamber once again. There are no rules about killing those unimportant to the narrative. At least not in the training video.

I muster my best Banzo voice in response.

"Coming! Hold your godforsaken horses, woman!"

Studying endless hours of tape on Banzo helps me approximate a reasonably accurate response. But my voice is hoarse, unsure. My vocal cords are still assimilating to this alcoholic sideshow vagrant's tone and pitch. The agony is barely containable.

But I've been through this before. At least once.

The Creators wipe our memories after two replacements. They only leave us with enough to fall back on for experience and reference. I might have already done this a thousand times. It would boggle my mind if I had the time to allow for such a thing.

A circus clown. My last switch was a housewife. Mother of four. Two boys. Two girls. They call that a billionaire's family. Ted from next door called it that. I enjoyed paring his flesh with a ceramic knife my in-laws gifted me for Christmas. It is a good memory. One I will be sad to see go once *this* switch is complete.

It is not wise to grow fond of the memories. They leave you as quick as the life leaving the body you're replacing.

The body. I simply cannot leave it in the closet for much longer.

But the show is about to start. My big performance. Sight gags, pratfalls, and communicating mis-understandings through a series of blinks. Who comes up with such buffoonery?

The Creators could have at least inserted me a little sooner so I could dispose of the body more efficiently. This apparently has been brought up to them multiple times, but the complainant always has their memory wiped, so it remains a moot point. Come to think of it, I have no idea how I even know this.

The woman bangs on my door again. Before she can finish whatever threat she lobs my way, I open the door. *Fling* it open. The look on my face is supposed to be annoyance. But maybe it is closer to intimidation? She scuttles off after a momentary glance.

Damn it all. My eyes. Have they changed yet? Are they still alien to these bags of impatient flesh? I rush back to my mirror to double check. No. My eyes belong to the clown.

Banzo had never been intimidating in his life. The door harpy picked up on something in my stare. I need to recede such aggression. Someone will catch on. Even if only subconsciously. The switch will be ruined.

I must focus. Relax. Breathe. I can hear muffled applause in the circus tent. Is it truly my time?

I make my way as faux-drunk as I can to the back door. Eyes eager to affix onto anyone who might suspect me of being false. But why would they suspect me? They have no grounds. I surmise no one pays attention to Banzo. Not even the kids in the crowd out there. This should be simple.

The show has indeed started. I peek my head out ever so slightly. The opening act is getting the crowd in the proper mood. A few jugglers. Some acrobats. One of the elephants shuffles around with a dull smile. Probably beaten into him as a permanent fixture.

A cold voice freezes my ears from behind me. The voice of a greedy, petulant man.

"You're up next. Finale ain't yours no more. Not after Topeka. Got to earn it back. Capiche?"

Topeka. What did this drunken fool of a clown do in Topeka? Think. Think, damn it all.

"Aw to Hell with Topeka. Wish I could forget that mess."

I slur my words just enough to make it seem convincing.

The man, Roland Benz, balks for a slight second. Does he suspect?

No. No, he doesn't. His brother, Mickey Benz is the flighty one. *He* would suspect. But he's nowhere to be seen. Probably in the female acrobats' dressing room. The lout. At least, that's what the training video said.

Roland only saw money. If Banzo wasn't drawing, Banzo was out of a job eventually. And that cannot happen. Not now. Time to ensure my longevity with a showstopping performance that the old Banzo could never pull off.

The woman squawks at me yet again.

So I go. My time in the spotlight. The switch depends on Banzo's act. On *my* act.

And then I will wait. Wait for the Benz Brothers Big Top Massacre of 1976 to unfold six months from now. Sure, we're a little early, but I know every detail by heart. Banzo won't save anyone this time. No reluctant hero. No sideshow hobo with a heart of gold. I have trained for this for what seems like an eternity. Anyone who stands in my way of ensuring one Allen Lee Ginter slaughters his way through that sold out show in Kansas City in six just months' time will join Banzo in the closet. In a manner of speaking, of course. It is the only way to appease the endless hunger of Chaos. That's *exactly* how the training video put it.

And chaos *must* be sown. The Creators demand it. Without it, this world is doomed.

It won't be long now. I must remove Banzo from that closet and Roland Benz will help.

After all, that's how the training video started.

NOTES

D&T Publishing originally released this in their bi-weekly newsletter. Initially, I felt it was just a fun little flash piece I could throw out and forget. But then, a lot of people got back to me and said they really loved this one. I returned to it to see what they were on about and I kinda agree now. The idea of doppelgangers being these interdimensional gremlins ready to sow chaos in service to a faceless master tickled me to no end. The whole videotape thing is just a cool piece of flair to put a sort of corporate master bow on it all. I really like the worldbuilding here and would definitely consider revisiting it as a novella or a screenplay. Who the fuck knows. Best of intentions and all that shit. Doppelgangers terrify me. I write about them a lot. In fact, there might be another one coming up later in your journeys here. I don't envy you one bit. Safe travels.

RECOMPENSE

The headache had returned.

I had hoped it would stay away a little while longer. The damned thing's voice scritch-scratched across the inside of my skull again; a persistent pain that dug a hole in my brain with razor-sharp words only I could hear.

"Daniel's innocence cannot get in the way of your vengeance. Our master plan."

Its rusted spike of a lilt made me curse the day I found that damned curio necklace. That faded gold-plated bauble seemed so innocent. So unassuming. Just lying there, all alone in that forgotten little secondhand shop. It was to be a gift for my Maxine. That was when I heard *it* for the first time. Reminding me of my failures in life. My betrayers and their continued existence. My inability to shield my loved ones from the random chaos of the universe. I hated its voice and craved its attention simultaneously.

So all-consuming was its voice, I had almost forgotten that I was still smack in the middle of the stark, cold office of my employer, Mr. Loomis.

"Are we set, Mr. Grover?" The paunchy, overly sideburned Mr. Loomis asked his assistant, but had his eyes on me the whole time.

"Yes. Yes, we are ready. Ready to take everything you hold dear as recompense."

I almost nodded in agreement as the thing's voice continued to claw a groove into my head bone.

"Not to worry, Mr. Loomis. We'll take care of everything," Mr. Grover replied. The thing's laugh echoed inside me as it anticipated what was to come.

As I took the black leather duffel bags filled with cash from Mr. Grover, all I could think of was how purple the sunset was that night. It bled through the floor-to-ceiling windows in Loomis' office like a silent, warm scream. I read somewhere that meant there was pollution in the air. How could something so beautiful come from something so disgusting? I don't even know if it's true. If it is, though, it makes me hate this world that much more.

Four million dollars in unmarked bills. Twenties and fifties. No hundreds. The ransomers were adamant about that. It rattled around in my head ever since we got the call. Were they afraid of the number one hundred? Maybe of triple digits? I wanted to ask Mr. Loomis about it. Maybe he had the same fear.

Mr. Grover was indeed Mr. Loomis' right-hand man, even though he was clearly left-handed. Mr. Loomis was insistent on Mr. Grover handing the money directly to the kidnappers alone, but I convinced them it was a good idea that I go along with Mr. Grover. For backup. In case anything might happen. The look on Mr. Loomis' face when I offered was one of panic and regret. I assured him in my own mute way that Grover and I together would ensure Daniel's safe return.

I'm usually a terrible liar but when it came to the safety of my own family, I could fib with the best of them. Maxine said she'd wait up for me tonight and I can't disappoint her. Not this time.

* * *

Oh, that shop. That accursed store where I found the necklace. I should have known to stay away from such a place. It smelled like old, dead things lived there. And they did. *Things* like that curio necklace. Long-forgotten demons and spirits nestled in the discarded items of the deceased. It made me nauseous just thinking about it.

48

Maxine had been getting weaker lately. More tired. I had precious little time with her while she was awake. I wanted to make the most of it. I knew a gift from the heart would help her recover. Give her resolve. I searched shop after shop for something that would save her. Rejuvenate her. And *that's* when I came across that accursed place. Deep in the old part of the city, where the people were just as disregarded as the crumbling architecture. You could almost hear the voices of the dead insisting they were once happy there.

It called to me. *It* tricked me. Even though I somehow knew going in there would be the beginning of my end. Hmph. It figured. The impetus for my grand plan of revenge just so happened to be my undoing. It's just as well. Maxine *will* be cared for. I've seen to it. All that remains is pure, unadulterated recompense. The damned thing will help me get it. And then it will take me straight to Hell. It hasn't said so, but I know how these things end. Nothing in life is free, especially revenge.

The necklace was the absolute perfect gift for Maxine. A simple two-photo curio with a rickety clasp and a longer-than-usual chain. She loved old things. Things owned by people long gone from this world. I didn't share her taste, but I knew exactly why she liked such things. The feeling of permanence. An item, a keepsake destined to remain here for as long as humans would bear its lifeless imposition. I knew it would lift her spirits even though just touching it made my skin crawl. In a way, I cleansed it for her as soon as I held it. I carried such a burden willingly while she remained alive and happy. She will stay that way. It promised me so.

When I asked the decrepit shopkeeper how much the necklace was, she said it was not for sale in an empty, paper-thin voice that begged for the sleep of death. She had to be at least ninety years old. What kept her there? Hanging on by *such* a tiny thread. Was it stubbornness? Or was it something else? Perhaps a need to warn others of what lay inside the possessions of the dead?

I had to have it, that curio. She was insistent on not selling it, though. Unfazed, I asked her why it was even on the sales floor in the first place. Her stammering excuse that it was never supposed to be out at all, and that she had no idea why, wasn't good enough for me. Like I said, I *had* to have it. Her empty voice filled quickly when she realized I would do anything for it. Anything. She proceeded to explain the history of the thing. Its terrible, misbegotten history. It passed from one owner to the next, bringing misery and misfortune like clockwork. When I asked who owned it originally, she gave me the most sheepish whimper a human could possibly muster. A nameless man who dabbled in all sorts of unholy things. He locked away something terrible within the curio that was never meant for human sensibilities. My smile did not dissipate one iota as she told all of this to me. I think that frightened her more than anything else. One man's foul luck is another's turn of the worm. I could feel opportunity knocking deep in my innards.

I soon left the shop as quick as could be. There were no other customers to be seen and no passersby to witness my exit. Fortuitous and suspicious at the same time. I knew I wanted the necklace, but the thing was insistent that I take it from her and crush her head like a rotted coconut with my bare hands. The fear in her eyes when I pocketed the necklace gave me the briefest of pauses. Was it more than just disgust at my brazen thievery? That's when I heard the thing's true voice for the first time.

"She knows not what I truly am. Open the clasp and see me."

It felt like a wet needle jabbing behind my eyes. Painful yet succulent. I shook my head out of sheer reflex and I swear the shopkeeper must have known it was in my head right then. I didn't give her time to utter neither warning nor admonition. The thing agreed that her head must implode. And so, it did. Nothing could keep me from making sure Maxine was happy. After all, I'm all she has now.

We're all she has now.

* * *

I'll never forget the night everything changed for us as long as I live. Which might not be much longer. Maybe they'll let me see my daughter's face in Hell. It would be better than the indifference of oblivion. Anything but that. I'd rather feel eternal torture than nothing at all. Maybe that's why I took the necklace in the first place. Now that it's inside of me, I never have to be alone when I'm away from Maxine.

That night. The night they took Maxine's mother away from her. From me. Mr. Loomis swore he would help me find the ones that did…*that*…to her. He'd help me get revenge. But I knew. I knew it was him. His appetites were insatiable. Oh, in public he was always on his best behavior. But in private, no worse savage animal has ever existed. As far as I know, Grover knows nothing. But he's good at keeping things close to his vest. Maybe he does know something after all. We *will* make him talk before it's all over.

Cara didn't deserve her fate at the hands of Loomis. I've never wavered on that sentiment. Yes, she coveted him. They saw each other. Multiple times. I watched every rendezvous just out of sight. But to her credit, she tried to break it off. I was willing to forgive her. That's what real love is, you know. Loomis, the narcissist, couldn't handle rejection. Even though he had gotten what he wanted, he still insisted on getting the last word.

The last word consisted of sending her decapitated head to our house in a box for Maxine to open while I was in the backyard mowing the lawn. The scream my daughter let out makes me wish for death daily. She hasn't spoken since. Not even after she got sick. Really sick. The doctors said it was stage four, but she was responding so well to chemo for a good long while. One doctor, an impudent penguin of a man, recommended hospice recently. I stabbed him in the shoulder with a pen and demanded a second opinion. She *will* live. Even before I met it, that thing, I knew she would live. That's real love, you know.

* * *

The thing. It tells me its name several hundred times a day. Like an automated recording. In case I somehow forget. *Decidit. Lapsus. Caducus.* Those are the ones I remember. The ones that stick in my head. Its voice is like metal scraping concrete while a child screams for its mother. I have grown used to it. Somewhat. When it's speaking to me, there's a certain agonizing comfort I get from it. When it's absent from my mind, when it sleeps, there is relief but also withdrawal. A terrifying void of uncertainty and neediness. His silence causes a chasm of violent paranoia in my soul. I'm not ashamed to say I crave it. It can't even be helped anymore. It sounds pathetic, I'm sure. But if you ever do hear its voice, there'll be no escape for you, either.

It knew my plan for revenge the moment it spoke to me. It motivated me to act instead of wallow in grief and apathy. I soon disappeared from the syndicate. Relocated. Moved myself and Maxine to the other side of the city. I didn't give them any time to find us. We were gone in the night. Soon after, I was recuperating from the plastic surgery I had insisted upon myself. I knew that had to be the catalyst of my plan for comeuppance. As I healed from the scalpel, I grew closer to Maxine than ever before. Even though she couldn't speak, I conversed enough for the both of us. I know in my heart she appreciated it. After the bandages came off, she was surprisingly understanding of the fact that her father no longer looked like her father. A benevolent stranger. My once kind, round features now replaced with a harsh, angular mask on the constant verge of a monumental sneer. I hoped it would ameliorate the flame-seared image in her mind of her mother's head. With my old face gone, another reminder of that horrific day was no more. I like to think that it helped. No matter, though. When the cancer came, she was virtually helpless and barely coherent most of the day. I was all she had, regardless of what current cowardly face I hid behind.

My plan was to start back at the bottom of the syndicate. Work my way back up. No longer was I humble, obedient Mr. Thorpe. I now called myself Mr. Marvin. And so would they. I knew they would recognize my voice, though, so I paid a retired prize fighter named Percy to crush my vocal cords with a pair of brass knuckles. I'm sure it was the easiest hundred dollars he ever made. I think he enjoyed it immensely if I'm being honest. The utter misanthrope.

So there we were, two mutes against the world, Maxine and I. Loomis and Grover (and the rest of the syndicate, for that matter) never suspected once who I really was. A thin-faced, silent thug; violently loyal to a fault and had no discernible backstory. I had no compunction about killing anyone now, innocent or guilty, so there was no way I would ever be suspected as a cop. If I could just keep Maxine safe, everyone else could burn for all I cared. I had just one job in life now and I wasn't about to let her down. Or *it*.

The thing. *Caducus. Decidit. Lapsus.* Whatever you want to call it. It knew immediately all I had endured. My endeavors. My desire. My plot. I think that's exactly why it bonded with me. A fallen demon mingling with a fallen wretch. Forgotten things. Shunned loyalty. It's almost beautiful if you think about it. No. It *is* beautiful. You'd know it if you were as blessed as me to have felt *it* inside you.

It helped me. Made my plan better. Made my revenge more streamlined. Efficient. Less emotional. Straight to the point. I must admit, even I blushed at its endgame. I was just planning on killing Loomis after an impassioned rant. But this. Oh my. It was what ghouls dreamed of while they slumbered in the corpses of the unloved.

I adored it. If you could indeed love something so terrible.

And I did.

*   *   *

When Loomis received the call that his son Daniel had been kidnapped, I struggled immensely to keep from laughing out loud in my own muffled, honking way. It would have ruined the whole thing.

The demon was impeccable at mimicking the ignorant, staccato mumblings of a low-level kidnapper. I granted him the free will to wreak havoc on my employer's life. The break from his demonic droning in my skull was a welcome respite, though I did crave its return just as much. Mr. Grover was apoplectic when the call came in. He was like a second father to Daniel. In fact, he was more like a first father to Daniel. What with Loomis' proclivities and rank selfishness taking up most of the man's time. Daniel was a spoiled child because of all that, but I still felt sorry for him. Children are a product of their environment. If he were my son, he'd be in a better position to be a good kid. Yes, even now. Maxine was an angel. We raised her right. I can say that with certainty. It's one of my true accomplishments in life. Unconditional love is a hell of a thing, you know.

The drop was to happen at one in the morning underneath the Delano Causeway. A seedy shanty town lurked there. Whores. Drugs. Plenty of angry poor people around to distract from our dealings. From what the thing had planned. As we drove, Grover cried. That kind of painful cry a man squeezes out when he's told all his life to suck it up and be a man. *Don't show weakness, boy.* It all comes to a head one day when your boss' kid gets kidnapped and you were powerless to stop it from happening even though you're closer to the boy than anyone else on the planet. That kind of cry. It was uncomfortable. Mr. Grover had a bushy, overhanging mustache that hid his mouth while it was shut. As he sobbed, close-mouthed, it almost looked as if a small animal was whining on his face. A pet he kept on his visage for some odd reason. I again had a hard time trying not to laugh. All this plotting and planning and a loose noise might be the death of me. That's apropos of life in general, I suppose.

I asked Grover why he was crying, and he told me he loved Daniel like a son. This was information I knew in my past life as the weak, vulnerable Mr. Thorpe. A listless voyeur spying on his wife's infidelities. Grover was never one to divulge anything about his private life. To the old me *or* the new me. Or to anyone else. It sounded gross when he said it, though. Regardless of whether he meant it to or not. They're not the same as Maxine and I. No one is.

The rest of the ride was quiet, save for a smattering of stifled sobs from Grover. He was trying so desperately to keep me from hearing them. He was failing and it now annoyed me rather than eliciting pity.

We arrived at the corner of Plainfield and Galax, right under the eastern ramp of the hulking, rotten Delano Causeway. A corpse of a bridge that was more of a symbol of this city's cankerous nature than a means of practical conveyance across Highsmith Bay. No matter. This was the *perfect* place to enact the next part of the plan. I got out first. Grover followed a moment later, no doubt trying to push down his emotions like a real man. I didn't care anymore. This was going to happen. I had convinced myself that Grover knew about Loomis and his vices. About Loomis and Cara. *My* Cara. Maybe he's the one who sent her head to our house. Just business, right? We were about to find out.

Each one of us grabbed two bags of the ransom money and placed them at our feet, as my skull-splitting voice of reason had instructed. Leave the trunk open, it said. Place the bags of cash at your feet, it said. Don't say a word, it said. And so on and so forth. I took a small amount of joy in just standing there with Grover, awash in awkward silence. Waiting for someone I knew wasn't coming. Waiting for something I knew wasn't going to happen. It felt nice. Therapeutic. The thing didn't say a word. But I could feel it smiling. Like a rotting cat breathing on the back of your neck in a pitch-black room. Its lips long decayed, leaving a rictus grin that would stain the soul of God itself.

After what felt like more than a suitable amount of time, I pulled my loyal revolver out of its shoulder holster and pistol-whipped Mr. Grover harder than he deserved at that moment. I almost knocked him out and cursed under my breath. I could feel the thing laughing softly at my zeal.

"Patience. Tonight is all you have left. Savor it."

Though we hadn't discussed my fate per se, I knew what he meant. He was right. I needed to slow down. With my gun trained on Grover, I offered my free hand for him to stand. He refused. Spit blood on my shoe.

"You out of your god damned mind? The hell was that for? Huh?"

His indignance was gratifying. He never expected to get bit from such a loyal hound. I had been waiting for this next part for a long time. Such a very long time.

I let it speak through me. It crunched its dying star, black hole of a voice through my dead vocal cords and forced a horrible sound through my long dormant mouth that mimicked the speech of a sentient hellhound. A flaming, lashing tongue; the sound of gurgling magma oozed from my maw. It nearly brought me to tears.

"You knew. Mr. Thorpe. His wife. Mr. Loomis. You knew everything. And you did nothing. And now you stand here, weeping for that boy like you deserve sympathy."

That's right. That is indeed what I used to call myself. Thorpe. Hearing his name made my ears flinch. I don't remember that man. He wouldn't like me now. And I wouldn't like him. It's for the better that Thorpe is dead and buried beneath Mr. Marvin.

Grover fell backwards at the sound of my voice. A voice manipulated by my benefactor. We were both fallen. Right then is when I truly felt we were helping each other up. Purpose itself is a potent drug. More than love. More than hatred. Unadulterated purpose. It's what humans truly crave. If Cara's fate gave me purpose, true purpose, then I would suffer her end a thousand times to feel this useful. This alive.

"What the fuck are you? How are you... How do you—?" Grover was flummoxed and near the precipice of a permanent mental break. I needed him to say it. Now.

"Admit what you did, and you shall be set free. Admit your part in Mr. Thorpe's unraveling. No one is coming to save you. Or Daniel."

I saw him nod. It was quick. Almost involuntary. But I saw it. And he saw me see it. His admission of guilt in the plot against my family. My very existence. It was all I needed.

I didn't even feel myself swoop down upon Grover and begin to tear him apart with my bare hands. Eviscerate him with my teeth. Slurp his blood. Suckle his marrow. It was all the thing's doing. It was driving me, so I didn't have to fret about the fatal details. The closest thing to a friend I've ever had.

You might think it sad, but it reminded me of the love I had for Maxine. Unconditional. Selfless.

Grover cried and screamed and gurgled like a real man that night. I wonder if Daniel heard any of it. After all, it was all for him no doubt.

* * *

Upon my brief return home, I had precious little time alone with Maxine. I still needed to confront Loomis for the big finale. Though I wasn't as excited about it as I thought I'd be even though that was the true end. This here was the interlude I had hoped for, though. Just her and I.

She was so quiet. So peaceful. I could see the faintest rise and fall of her chest. She was still there, ever so slightly. I shared a long, silent witching hour with her, just sitting next to her as she slept. I finally gathered up enough courage to give her the curio necklace. I had inserted a picture of myself and of Cara in it so we could be close to her heart always. I spied my picture briefly as the rickety clasp gave way and opened. Was that Thorpe or Marvin? I couldn't remember which one she wanted or was appropriate. I had no idea anymore. I placed it in her hand. It was cold. I shook her gently more out of politeness than surprise. I knew. I had waited too long. I should have roused her, health be damned. I sat there, her hand in mine, and the way the moonlight came through the window behind her bed and shone onto her pale, sickly skin was a weird comfort. It made me smile and I'm not quite sure why.

It was then I realized what the thing meant when it said Maxine would be taken care of.

At least eternal damnation was off the table for her. Was oblivion really the only other option? Was that the trick of heaven? The void? I laughed out loud with a crooked, painful croak at the cleverness of the fallen thing inside my head. Well played.

I sat for a little while longer in her quiet, frigid room and just stared at her. She was beautiful, stuck like that for as long as the rot would let her. I kissed Maxine's hand and then affixed the curio necklace to her stiffening neck. It looked absolutely perfect on her. There was one last thing that had to be done and I was certain it would still happen in Mr. Thorpe's basement. No. Mr. Marvin's basement. Yes. Marvin. He's the one who lives here.

"Thorpe is dead. He does not dwell here. The dead have no cares for your temporary discomfort."

* * *

I felt nothing as I brought Daniel's head to Mr. Loomis. I didn't even stuff it in a box. I just held a clump of his hair in my clammy fist and strolled in. The blood had long since drained from it. Most of it currently pooled on the passenger side floor of Mr. Grover's car. As I marched to the elevator leading to Loomis' penthouse, I was sure I was smiling. Grinning ear-to-ear. But a quick glimpse in a lobby mirror showed I was crying. My face red and raw with the tears of that weakling Thorpe. How could that be? I'd never felt so alive in my life. I had purpose. I had approval from a power above us. An ant validated by a magnifying glass; sunbeams be damned.

When I finally reached his office, his son's head still firmly in hand, Loomis went through all the expected initial emotions. Confusion. Anger. Belligerence. Soon after, I simply dropped his son's head to the floor. The coconut-like sound it made when it hit triggered a deep shock inside of Bransford Digby Loomis III. Eater of men. Devourer of industry. Scion of capitalism. He dropped to his knees. Sobbing. Wailing. Screaming. Then came the questions.

The demands. Who was I really? What did I want? And others of the sort. I received no joy from his soul pouring forth uncontrollably. No satisfaction. Maxine was safe. Cara was long dead. Was I really doing this for them? Did I expend everything on Grover? Have I nothing left to savor? The night was ending and that meant so was I. The thing dug its claws into my soul, ready to rip it from my body and offer it to the Morningstar as a prize. A bargaining chip to return to the good graces of an infernal realm that held no gentle circumstances for me. I inhaled sharply. It was the worst pain I had ever felt in my life, yet I appreciated the scream of every one of my tortured nerve endings.

Mr. Marvin was now damned for Mr. Thorpe's apathetic existence. I barely remember being Thorpe anymore. Even my memories of Maxine were as Marvin. The ones that mattered, the thing tells me. Will I be tortured for all eternity as Thorpe or as Marvin? Does it even matter anymore?

I glanced at another mirror, in hopes of seeing Mr. Thorpe. Even just a glimmer of him. What I saw instead was the sneering, horned visage of the thing. Leering at me. Broken teeth, amber eyes, rotting jaw. Like an ember-kissed, emaciated bull bound for hell and relishing the thought of it.

I smashed the mirror with my feeble hand. Thorpe's hand. Seeing the thing in the flesh was too much all at once. I knew it mustn't have anything near a pleasant visage, but fantasy and reality really do make terrible bedfellows. I picked up a large shard of the reflective glass with my shredded, crimson hand and sliced off jagged chunks of my face without a single ounce of ceremony. Marvin's face. I lobbed them one by one at a sobbing Loomis. My bloody flesh sticking to his tear-stained face as he crawled away from me on his marble office floor. Blood smears making hard squeaking noises as he scrambled backwards. His cries sounded like an orphaned toddler's death rattle. He was once someone I looked up to. Someone to whom I *wanted* to remain loyal. Now he was just as useless as Grover. And Thorpe.

"Is this Marvin or Thorpe? Is it Marvin?! Or is it Thorpe?! You were supposed to be my purpose, but I feel nothing!" I screamed at him as I hurled the last of my face at his quivering body. Loomis was finished. Broken. Stammering and crying with not a sound coming from his mouth. Now he must know what it feels like. I was sure Maxine would approve. There was nothing left behind his eyes. Killing him would only ease his suffering. The thing was satisfied. It scratched its sharp hooves against my skull. It wanted to go home. It was time.

I only received one warning of what was about to happen.

"Are you ready, Mr. Marvin?"

And there it was. Thorpe was saved. I was sure of it. I was afraid to ask, but I was sure of it.

I had no time to say anything. Think anything. Do anything. There was little point in it anyhow.

I did, however, catch a brief glimpse of the sun coming up as the thing dragged me to Hell by my dead vocal cords, laughing softly all the way. The sunrise had that same purple haze, just like at last sunset. Surprisingly, I didn't hate a single thing about it.

NOTES

Whenever I try to write something super-serious, I subconsciously end up writing dark comedy after dark comedy. This story is the closest you'll get from me as far as a serious piece of short fiction in the realm of horror. I'm too cheeky and flippant to buckle down and focus on the drama a lot of the times. It originally appeared in 2021 in the anthology *The Dire Circle*, from D&T Publishing. Basically, it's the reverse Zodiac or the Black Zodiac, if you will. I knew little about the evil Zodiac, so it was fun to read about it all and craft a story from one of the twelve nefarious signs. This one was centered around the Fallen Demon. A being determined to swing things back in their favor, usually by manipulating a human to do their bidding. Combine that with a revenge story as bleak as the UK weather, and there you have it. Some people have told me they get a Clive Barker vibe from this, and I can't say I disagree after rereading this and comparing it with some of his short work. There could be worse comparisons! There's a lot of mob revenge movies mixed with supernatural vengeance comics and fiction here to be sure. This is another one I wouldn't mind expanding upon one fine day.

IT WAS PROBABLY JUST THE WIND

Inside the tiny office of Braid Brothers Realty, behind a tiny, dented metal and wood grain teacher's desk from a tiny school built in the 1960s, sits tiny little Beto Braid. A nebbish, squirrely man stuck in his mid-forties with all kinds of facial tics. His older brother, the much more inoffensive-looking and sturdier backboned Belfast Braid, is at a realtor's conference in Kalamazoo. Not enough in the petty cash for two to travel. And so, the hunch of a man saddled with being the Younger Mr. Braid resides here. Alone. Trapped with the clientele in all their rigorous glory. One of his many well-worn facial tics includes one that makes his visage appear as if it were trying to escape his perpetually shrugging face altogether in a mad panic. Such a countenance is mainly and currently brought on by the couple sitting across from him in different-colored metal folding chairs. Their energy is simultaneously menacing and idiotic.

The husband, Freddie Krinkle, is a beady-eyed man with a very punchable face and a tacky plaid suit. The wife, Cath Smithers-Krinkle, is a nattily dressed woman with a blank expression and eyes way past the point of exhaustion or caring. About anything. She grips the free water bottle Beto gave her like it's her only lifeline. Freddie has already thrown his half-empty one on the floor. The Younger Mr. Braid looks through his finger-smudged glasses at them whilst holding a stack of rumpled documents with a shaky hand.

"You *are* aware that this house is haunted, correct."

"Allegedly," Freddie scoffs.

"No, I mean it's really haunted. I was thrown out of a second story window while I was completely alone. I very much almost died."

The Younger Mr. Braid is clearly still shaken from this experience and gets a faraway look not uncommon to those affected by PTSD. He whimpers a little, like a frightened puppy. Freddie flinches at the noise. His empathy meter was never installed at birth.

"Hmph. Probably a loose board. You shouldn't run like that in old houses. You're lucky to be alive," Freddie chides the Younger Mr. Braid with a tutting chuckle. The air in the room has turned a lumpy texture of awkward.

Cath offers a calming hand on Freddie's shoulder, which he ignores. Par for the course in the Smithers-Krinkle household, wherever that may be at the moment.

"Fred—"

"What I mean is that I *am* aware, and I am very excited about it."

Braid narrows his eyes more than a little.

"Uh... You are?"

"Excited about writing it off on my taxes, that is."

Freddie elbows Cath playfully, but a little too hard. She gives him a tired smile and an almost silent wheeze.

"*Our* taxes," Cath corrects him.

"Sure. Sure."

"I don't follow," the Younger Mr. Braid squeezes his voice through a noticeable frown.

Cath sighs. "He hosts a ghost skeptic show on TikTok. It's called SkepToks. It's popular. Do you TikTok?"

She does the air quotes with her fingers when she says "popular."

"No. And I don't 'get up stop' either," Braid grimaces.

Neither Freddie nor Cath laughs at his Color Me Badd joke.

"That's a reference from the 90s. Do you know where that is?" Braid asks sincerely.

"Oh, and he also fucks the house," Cath mumbles under her already mumbly breath, but still hoping the Younger Mr. Braid hears her nonetheless.

"I'm sorry, what?" Beto Braid just wobbles back and forth like he's an inflatable bobble toy that a toddler just pie faced.

"Thank heavens for no contingencies! Oh boy! Now where do I sign?" Freddie claps his hands and rubs them together with something way past vigor before he glances at Cath. That prompts her to retrieve a pen from her tastefully displayed cleavage.

The younger Mr. Braid looks askance at both of them, incredulous.

"You *are* aware that this house is haunted, correct? Correct? Yes?"

It's all he can muster behind his tiny desk in that tiny office with his tiny voice.

* * *

The drive from Braid Brothers Realty to the house consisted of thirty minutes of listless silence and ten minutes of Freddie trying to remember the lyrics to "Captain of Her Heart" at the top of his bent accordion lungs.

And then there it is. *The deal of the century*. At least, that's what the Senior Mr. Braid said on the phone. No catches. Just deals. His voice didn't shake or waiver or at all when he said it.

Freddie and Cath park their car diagonally and impudently in the massive gravel driveway of a massive 1840s house in alarmingly great condition. Blue with cream trim. Gigantic front porch, huge sunroom in the rear. Three stories plus an attic and a basement. A seemingly endless flower garden out back. Emerald green lawn all over. Just lovely.

"Doesn't look that scary," Freddie huffs as his hands search for his hips.

From a small window in the attic, a most likely dead woman with hollow black eyes in a tattered, dirty white gown points menacingly at them. Her mouth locked in a painful frown of someone betrayed at the most inopportune moment possible.

Cath spots her with a slight double take.

"Uh, there's a dead woman in the attic window."

"What? No, there's not."

"She's right there. She's clearly pointing at us."

"I don't see anything. You're *clearly* stressed out from the move. Maybe you should lie down."

"I feel fine, I—"

Freddie pushes her toward the house.

"In you go, silly. Oh man, the things I'm gonna do to this place. Her knees are gonna be weak for weeks."

"Try not to leave any stains out in the open, Freddie. My mom is insisting on visiting as soon as we're settled."

"Fuck her. Let's go christen this place. You record like usual. 'Kay?"

"'Kay."

The dead woman in the attic is still staring at them and Cath keeps her eyes on the ghoul as Freddie ushers her inside with a poking finger and a swooshing noise dipped in patronizing disdain.

Cath attempts a half-wave at her.

The dead woman waves right back.

Cath 'hmphs' to herself in passive wonderment.

"What was that?" Freddie inquires brusquely.

"I said we should get gas station sushi later."

"Great idea! You're good for a few of them here and there after all. Home sweet home here we come! In more ways than one, eh?"

*   *   *

Moving in is the easy part for the Krinkles. A bunch of Ikea furniture, a few heirlooms, and a whole lot of nothing. They travel light on account of Freddie falling in love with a new potentially haunted house every eighteen months or so. A full library of books and movies and a complete set of cookware just gets in the way of a good, solid abode penetration.

A few weeks after their arrival, late at night, around quarter past three, the ghoulish attic specter materializes in their bedroom and lifts up her own dress, revealing an ectoplasmic bush of pubic hair covering her deceased vagina. There's no lasciviousness in her exhibition. Just very matter-of-fact. An invitation? Saucy indeed. Maybe a warning, perhaps? But what the hell kind of warning is that? Cath, after complimenting the expired woman's poltergeisty pubic area, politely suggests she drop her gown and engage her in a more ladylike fashion. After that initial dramatic entrance, they end up talking for hours as Freddie snores like a pig with a slit throat. Her name is Melina. Kincaid. A nice name for an allegedly vengeful spirit. She tells Cath about her murder and the subsequent revenge on her philandering husband and how she's become connected to the house. She can feel and sense people's emotions when they're inside. Pretty banal stuff, all told. Cath tells her she hoped for something a little more salacious, which offends Melina more than a little. Melina then blurts out she thinks she's in love with Cath and Cath being so insensitive to her ghost origin story is making her rethink things on that matter. The only thing Cath says in return is that if she is indeed connected to the house, she should prepare for Freddie to drill a few holes in the wall for some panky without the hanky. After a few more minutes of awkward shifting around in the conversation

67

amid attempts at small talk that die in the crib before it can crawl, Melina just disappears into thin air.

"Disapparated," Cath says aloud as Freddie continues to gag on his own snores.

* * *

Weeks go by. Melina is persona non grata. Spectera non grata? Cath is at the dining room table one random, lonely weeknight, catching up with busy work on her laptop. Her Etsy store is blowing up. Handcrafted ghost dolls that bear a striking resemblance to Melina are blowing up, more specifically, and she's having a hard time keeping them in stock. Bookkeeping from hell is the order of the day for her every day. She barely has any time to give a shit about Freddie and SkepToks. She used to be a regular on the show. Same goes for Freddie's new OnlyFans show, Ghost O-Face, the fetish series where he finds new ways to fuck the current old mansion he's in while it's purportedly haunted. There's a fetish for everything and this is one of the more popular ones. People in the know call it "EVP" for Extremely Victorian Penismanship. Business is apparently booming for him too. His holes have been discreet so far; one in the downstairs bathroom, a few in the walk-in closet, but soon discreet will no longer be a suitable word for his EVP setups.

Behind Cath is a long, dark hallway leading to the front of the house. Shadows from outside trees rest ominously throughout its length. One lone candle on a side cabinet. As she works, something appears from around the corner at the other end of the hallway and creeps toward her, getting closer from the background to the foreground. She looks up, stops typing, listens for something. Goes back to working. The thing creeps into the same room as her, almost on top of her. She turns around just in time to

68

see it as it lunges for her. It's wearing a tattered white nightgown.

"Melin—"

Freddie lies in bed, watching a ghost hunting show with a respectable erection. He's slowly kneading it with the knuckles of his pointer and ring finger through his royal blue satin pajamas.

"This Bagans guy is such a prude."

He hears a blood-curdling scream from downstairs. Freddie puts the show on mute.

"Did you take your anti-anxiety medication? You know how you get, crazypants!" He calls down with barely a care amidst his nasally honk of a shout.

He waits for a response. Nothing.

"Fine. Be that way," he harrumphs to himself.

He un-mutes the show and hums like a doofus as he resumes his dick kneading.

"Seduce that clown motel wall, Zack. Just flipping do it."

*   *   *

It's just a few days later and Freddie and Cath are on the couch, watching a movie together in the gloom of a freshly settled sun. Freddie is the picture of luxury and relaxation. Smoking jacket and slippers on. Munching popcorn, sipping champagne. Chortling at the movie they're watching.

Cath looks horrible. Possessed by something unspeakable. Or Melina. Heaving and breathing heavy, eyes bulged and bloodshot, sputum oozing from her crooked mouth. A nasty grunting gurgle coming from somewhere deep inside her.

Freddie laughs uproariously at the decapitation scene in *Hereditary* and offers popcorn to Cath without even looking at her. Cath's spastic fits increase as she stares down Freddie and knocks away the popcorn with a primal scream. Freddie finally looks at Cath and sighs.

"I told you not to get that California roll. Supermarket seafood is the dirt worst. Now look at you."

Cath lets out an awful bellow-howl right in Freddie's face. The smell is of rancid goat milk and baby vomit. He almost gags to completion.

"And now I'm completely flaccid. Thanks for that, hun. Is this your time of the month already? I feel like that *just* happened. Do you need a cuddle?"

Cath projectile vomits blood right in Freddie's face. He tags a chunk of thick red gunk with his tongue and smacks his lips.

"Huh. *Definitely* food poisoning."

Freddie calls someone on his phone, still drenched in bloody puke.

"Hey, it's me. Do you still make house calls? …Yeah, new house… Oh yeah, sexy as hell."

*　*　*

Shortly after Freddie makes the call, he's forced to strap Cath to their brand new four post bed complete with Egyptian cotton canopy. Very sheik, very upper middle class. Whatever possesses Cath is now rotting her skin like a bubbling cheese pizza left in a brick oven a few minutes too long and making her smell like shit still trapped inside of a dead cow's ripped-off torso.

A portly, goateed doctor in his forties, Dr. Bart, and an elderly skeleton of a priest with a ponytail, Father Plimpkin, stand at the foot of the bed next to a mumbling Freddie.

"Is this really necessary?" Freddie finally pipes up beyond a low rumble, lifting his head from his hands.

"You said this was food poisoning," Dr. Bart says with a protracted sigh.

70

"Exactly."

"Look, I'm as atheist as they come and even I can tell your wife is possessed by a fucking demon."

"Yeah, but did you have to call a darn priest of all things?"

"I mean, I can totally leave. No problem," the frail Father Plimpkin says plainly.

"Burn in Hell, scrotum-sucking, prick-licking arse-fuckers!" Cath's voice has changed to a cockney coal miner with acid reflux for some odd reason.

"Jeez, the language. I mean, I can handle the loose morals but the language, guys. Can't the menstrual cycle be responsible for this kind of attitude?"

Doctor Bart just stares at Freddie with a confused look.

"We should probably start the ritual before she kills us all. Like right now," Father Plimpkin almost whispers to himself like it wasn't even the reason they're all there.

"Well, I guess it can't hurt. I've heard exorcism can double as effective psychotherapy. Right?" Freddie chuckles as he gives his guests each a poke in the ribs with his bony elbows.

"How do you know this guy?" Plimpkin asks.

The good doctor shrugs. "We used to work retail together."

Father Plimpkin whips out a large wooden cross from his cassock and holds it out in front of him with more than a little pizzazz.

"In the name of Jesus Christ...!"

* * *

The night is full of blood, puke, protestations, levitations, incantations, and late-night pizza delivery. Freddie threatens to divorce and get back together with Cath seven times. He perforates the bedroom walls with a medium-sized Philips head screwdriver three times to make holes to fuck and records his orgasm face for SkepToks, completely ignoring the intense exorcism happening behind him. It's just background flavor.

The possessor's name is revealed to be Melina herself, jealous of Freddie getting to have Cath instead of her. She professes her love for Cath whilst inside of Cath which only annoys Freddie. Father Plimpkin refuses to believe it's an evil human spirit and insists on guessing every demon name in the book. Whatever book that is.

After Plimpkin leaves in frustration and boredom, Dr. Bart suggests that maybe Melina might try to win over Cath another way. A more sensible way, perhaps? Shortly after that, Melina's evil presence seems to subside completely. Dr. Bart, exorcist at large. Who would've thunk it.

Freddie and Bart say their goodbyes with promises to appear on SkepToks together and the house itself seems to sigh at that proposition.

Cath rests comfortably in their ravaged bed. Worn out and exhausted but safe. And alive. Freddie sits on the edge of the bed, doing his best impression of doting on her.

"That was crazy, right? I think I got some of it on SkepToks!"

"I think I was a slave to Satan."

"In a way, I suppose that's true."

Cath frowns a smidge, then turns it into a sly smile.

"Honey, could you get me a glass of water?"

"Sure, sweetheart. Practice your breathing exercises while I'm gone. You don't want to relapse into mental illness again, my silly!"

"'Kay."

She fake smiles at him.

Freddie jogs to the top of the stairs and notices a loose floorboard near the top step.

"Huh. Where the heck did that come from?"

An otherworldly voice echoes in the hallway. Female. Throaty. Cockney?

"FUCK... OFF..."

"Pardon me?"

An invisible force pushes him down the stairs like a strong gust of wind knocks a toddler into oncoming traffic. To his death. Him and the toddler.

"SHE'S... MINE..." The voice trails off into nothingness.

Cath, still in bed, waits for her glass of water with a gentle yet impatient hum.

"Hun...? Are you talking to someone?"

Nothing.

"Freddie...?"

Freddie's ghost races into the room, waving his hands all over the place. See-through yet glowing and smudged. Yelling at Cath breathlessly.

"Can you believe that phony realtor? Loose floorboards everywhere and he wants to blame it on ghosts! I am going to sue the pants off that joker. The nerve! It's going to get ugly. We should have asked for his brother. What was his name? Bravo? Biff?"

Cath can't see him but can tell something is in the room with her.

"Anyone there? Freddie? Water?"

"I'm right here! Hello?! Are you giving me the cold treatment now? The ol' silent shoulder? Fine, I'll let you be on the show again. Belfast! That's it. What a stupid name. Oh, forgot your water. Be right back, silly!"

Ghost Freddie trudges off to get ghost water in a ghost glass?

"Huh. It was probably just the wind," Cath says in Melina's voice.

NOTES

This one started as a very short screenplay and won a few awards and placed in a few competitions but that's about it. Unless you plan on making it yourself, short scripts have a very "short" shelf life. I just wanted to do a ridiculous take on haunted house and possession movies (which I can't get enough of, by the way) featuring a couple that can barely stand each other at this point in their relationship. It's also about the hypocrisy that is the relationship between belief and skepticism. Hardcore skeptics are just as annoying as hardcore believers. You don't want to be stuck in a room with either one as they are simply insufferable. Skeptics switch to believers and believers switch to skeptics all the time. Having the wherewithal to be flexible (in all aspects of life) makes you a better person. Point blank. Also, it's fun to want to fuck a possessed house. Make a hole and get to work. I still have a hankering to turn this one into a short film someday. Maybe sooner rather than later. We'll see.

IN HERE, WITH US

It's not as claustrophobic as you might think; We are quite comfortable as a matter of fact.

We see everything. We hear everything, too.

Oh, the priests and the deacons. They think we can't hear them as they whisper about us just out of what they think is earshot. We heard them talking the other night about what to do with us. Who to send. Someone from the Vatican, of all places. Someone experienced in these matters.

Good. Send them.

You would think we've grown bored of these parishioners and their vague transgressions. And you would be right. Humans aren't as unique as they think they are. Sure, there are variations of voice and behavior. Different smells. But their transgressions are all the same for the most part. Their confessions are interminably mundane. Their lazy, unimaginative sins. Afraid of leaving any minutiae out once inside with us. We ignore whichever priest is present at the time. We know they're really talking to *us*.

Oh, it was all some fun at first, we will admit. Making the confessional bleed. Pretending to be the voice of a trusting padre on the other side when none was present to begin with. It gave us great pleasure to plant such gleeful corruption in the midst of all this nauseating austerity.

Mmmmm. But how did we come to be here? Why are we allowed to endure in such a sacred place?

Wouldn't you like to know.

Although some of our kin delight in occupying the innocent, we on the other hand revel in long-term visitations of the depraved. The bloodthirsty. We like to see how much farther we can push them. With one Albert Dinwiddie, we believe we pushed too far. How were we supposed to know he was going to march straight into a church? We were certain he was headed to the liquor store. It was there in his mind. Chugging cheap vodka and name brand cranberry juice was his favorite pastime. On the way to dull his senses with booze, he took a stiff left turn into this gaudy monument to your god and his sacrificial lamb of a son. Didn't even signal he was about to do so. We couldn't predict it. Some might say we've lost a step in the last five hundred years or so. Maybe we have.

Maybe we have…

Yet we endure still. In here. Safe. Ensconced. Though unable to leave on our own accord.

We can hear them talking again in the rectory. Talking about *us*. Who we could possibly be. What our name might be. The expert from the Vatican has arrived in country. Touched down, as it were. One of the priests says he will pick them up from the airport. The other priest tells him to be careful. Ironic, considering whoever is left with us is the one in true danger. Maybe we will slay him after we poison his mind in a fit of hysteric madness.

The priest, the older, fatter one, says he will leave shortly. The younger, jangly priest says he will prepare for their return.

Good. Let him come. Let them prepare.

Let us do battle. We've been dying to stretch our legs for some time now. Maybe we will conduct some preparations of our own. Or maybe we shall just rest and let them do all the work. We are so very tired indeed.

We could do it, though. Oh yes, we could. We could flay the flesh from their bones with but a thought. We could pull their brains through their eye sockets with but a word. We could send them screaming straight to Hell with but a smile. All we need do is desire it.

Where were we? Oh yes, Albert Dinwiddie. We were so annoyed with his detour into this…place. What was it called again? Saint Something of Something or Other. Sacred Orgasming Heart of Our Lady's Rectal Warts. They all sound the same to us. We can't fathom how you pigs can tell any of them apart. McMansions for false devotion. Just as long as you don't get sentenced to *our* lord's domain, you'll try to get away with anything, and we mean anything, and then think apologizing to a lush pervert in a cassock will make it all better.

Idiots.

Then again, it's just in your nature. How you were made.

We should be steeling ourselves for the coming battle. We must focus.

We can hear the bony, jangly priest getting ready for our little confrontation. Donning his stole. Dusting off the old Roman Rituals. Bet that hasn't been used around here in a while. Or ever. We have half a mind to snuff out all of the candles in this dump and animate the life size Christ on the cross at the altar to stalk the skeletal padre in the dark. Make it whisper delightful obscenities in his ear. When the other priest returns with the alleged macaroni exorcist, this one will be nowhere to be found. Gone. Left the vicinity. It would be enough to scare the Pope into retirement. A grand act of terror. We think it would be exquisitely effective.

We just need to work up to it. Stretch the proverbial legs, as it were.

Give us time. These things take patience and willpower. Something you fleshbags know little about.

Ah yes, we know all about your daily regimen of vice and neglect. We've heard it all and then some. It's hard not to when you're trapped in this gloom box, prisoner to the mumblings of every poorly dressed mortal monkey that waltzes in and their uninspired ideas of what constitutes sin.

Cheating on your spouse. Wanting to cheat on your spouse. Wanting your spouse to cheat on you while you're in the room. Hating your children. Wishing they were dead. Wishing you were the one to do it. Not actually going through with it, though.

Oh, and there's masturbating too much, eating too much, doing too many drugs, not doing enough drugs, wishing you could rob a bank, wishing someone would rob a bank so you could save innocent bystanders and land your own reality TV show. Some of the things you walking sacks of failure come up with boggle the mind.

The killers. The rapists. The megalomaniacs. The world-eaters. They don't go to church. They have no illusions of who they are and what they want. They don't pretend to care if they're saved or damned or whatever. They know what they want now and aren't afraid to take it. *That's* the energy we feed off. We crave that kind of suckling. There's none of that to be had here, so our day consists of plotting, planning, and copious amounts of napping.

The other day, a young girl came in and confessed she hated her brother so much she wanted to push him in front of a car when he took her phone away from her. You animals and your technology. You covet it more than another's life or their company. What does a nine-year-old need with a pocket computer anyways? Unbelievable. We think her name was Rebecca. A nice child. Utterly boring in every way. Her greatest sin is being a selfish simpleton in a sea of selfish simpletons. It will only get worse as she grows older.

The priest is out of his office now. Hemming and hawing over whether he should come straight to us or bless the rest of the church first. His fear is odd. Mixed with unsteady resolve. He might not run if we pull out the freeze-tag-with-whispering-Jesus gag. Maybe the fat one will. We could stop his heart with but a laugh. That might scare the others into leaving. Or it could backfire horribly for us, and they could rally to fight us even harder.

It's too much to process. So many possibilities. We feel like we should have taken a good, long nap earlier. Now we'll be tired going into this titanic confrontation in a church no one gives a damn about. Probably won't even make the news if we kill all three of them. Everyone will think it's a hoax. A publicity stunt funded by the Catholic Church. There's a healthy number of cynics and atheists these days. Makes our job of seduction and corruption easier. We don't need anyone to believe anything to make us strong or something like that. Sounds like stupid fairy tale logic to us. This all should make for a good paranormal documentary someday, though. We always find those to be immensely entertaining.

There we go on another tangent.

When this all started, when Albert Dinwiddie entered this box to confess his sins, imagined or not, he had a complete break with reality and his mind collapsed into a pile of jabbering lunacy. He wasn't making any sense. The priest couldn't get anything out of him. It was a mess.

So, we exploded his head for making us come here in the first place.

Now that was the *real* mess. It was glorious.

We felt we had found our calling. Targeting unsuspecting fools in a trap of their kind's own making. But the joke was on us, as we know we have already stated. No psychopaths. No true evil. With the absence of genuine malevolence came the waning of my abilities. At first, we were able to take care of business, as it were. Soon though, all of that dried up.

The priest has returned with the exorcist. Two car doors slam just outside. No footsteps just yet. We can smell them. The Roman reeks of patchouli and stromboli. A disgusting combination. The fat priest's heart is racing. He knows what lies ahead. We could explode it with but a stare if we choose to manifest in full.

Or we could just take a quick power nap. Maybe they'll have lunch before we start things up.

After all, we are so very tired.

NOTES

I had intended to submit this to a monthly flash fiction contest way back when in 2021 when the subject was "haunted confessional booth." My mind raced with the possibilities, and I wrote a whopping 300 words. Cut to a year later and I finished it for myself and for this collection. Aren't you a lucky fucking duck? Anyhoo, I just thought the idea of a demon who thinks a little too highly of itself getting stuck inside a confessional booth without the foggiest of how to get out was the bee's knees. As with a lot of my stuff, it's a mix of dark and funny and it just can't be helped anymore. I've made peace with who I am as a writer. This book is part of that therapy. A bit of useless trivia for you, Albert Dinwiddie is the name of the escaped cannibal killer in our short film *What's For Dinner?* released in 2017. Check it out if you can find it online still. You get to see me in a fetching turtleneck and a nice shot of Chad's ass, so there's that as incentive.

ME, THE JURY

The near future. It's a deceptive term. Seems far away just by the sake of the slow march of the days of an average human being, but it always pounces on you sooner than you expect or are comfortable with. In our own near future, major criminal trials dealing with the most heinous of human deeds are decided a little differently than they are today.

It's all about what's on the menu during the first day of deliberation for the jury. Oh, it's not any kind of menu you can get at your local trough. This is a very unique kind of menu. Food is rarely even on it. And when it is, it's quite the special occasion.

With the advent of this menu, deliberations rarely ever go past that first day…

In a courthouse both familiar and foreign to us, in a sleek, overly metallic and angular deliberation room, with a long, recycled plastic table and twelve recycled plastic bucket chairs, reside our jury. Eight of them dead bodies. Some still in their chairs. Some slumped over the table. Others splayed out on the floor. Their causes of death range anywhere from gunshot wounds to the head, to multiple stabbings, to blunt force trauma. Blood smudges, smears, and spatters mar the once antiseptic room. A florescent light bulb in the ceiling flickers violently.

Amongst the dead are but four still alive:

Juror Two is a squirrely, fidgety young man with a thin face and small head. Eyes constantly darting around. His voice a high-pitched whine.

Juror Six is a calm, almost comatose-on-her-feet young woman. Judgmental eyes, slight mocking smile.

Juror Nine. A muscular, middle-aged man. Handsome. Emotionless, expressionless. His face and hands caked in blood.

An elderly man, Juror Eleven, has a look of disgust and outrage on his face. His left forearm bandaged tightly - the bandage stained a deep red.

"Are you proud of yourself? Did that feel good?" Eleven scolds Nine with a raspy hiss.

Juror Eleven glances over at a middle-aged woman at the head of the table. Dead in her chair from a steak knife to the throat. Juror One. Their forewoman.

Above them all in the corner between the ceiling and the wall, a holographic crawl repeats the same thing over and over:

"PLEASE REMAIN CALM AND PRO-FESSIONAL. PLEASE REFRAIN FROM ANY AND ALL PERCEIVED MICRO-AGRESSIONS."

"Don't kid yourself. You didn't like her, either. Self-righteous piece of—"

Two interrupts Eleven's attempt at a rant.

"Who? Him or her?"

"Take your pick."

Juror Six snorts a sharp laugh.

"What's next, boys? I don't have all day."

"Yeah, you do. That's the whole point of jury duty, idiot," Eleven says as he shakes his head.

Juror Two, seated next to Juror One's body, picks up one of the many long, thin laminated sheets of paper strewn about the room:

Each piece of paper features the heading **"JUROR ELIMINATIONS PROCESS MENU"**

Beneath that are a cryptic list of "entrees" such as:

"BREAKFAST MELEE"

"PSYCHOKINETIC PSYCHO-ANALYSIS"

"TEATIME CONFESSIONS"

"LIGHTNING ROUND TRANSACTIONAL ANALYSIS"

He slides his finger down the menu, past a few selections until his finger stops on one in particular:

"Morality Roulette," he mumbles.

"Great. More guns and knives, I assume?" Two quips.

The door to the outside flings open and a burly fifty-something bailiff who smells like stale pizza and too much Brut glides in with of all things a seemingly lifeless adult woman in an expensive pantsuit cradled in his arms. Powder blue jacket and pants. Pistachio blouse, kelly green pumps. Very stylish.

No, not a woman. Not a real woman, that is. A mannequin? A sex doll? An android?

The four remaining jurors eye her with surprise and total silence.

The husky bailiff pushes Juror One out of her chair and her body thwumps to the floor with a slight clonk as her head hits a split second after.

"What the fuck is this?" Nine asks with his hand firmly on hips.

"You prefer the gun?" asks Six.

"No, it's just—" Nine stammers, giving the bailiff enough time to rebuff him.

"Do what she says and don't make me come back in here. Yeah?" The bailiff growls with a throatful of phlegm.

"Oh goodie," Two drones.

"This should go smoothly," Eleven matches Two's sarcasm and their eyes meet involuntarily with a wink and a slight smile.

"Oh, like it did with Eight? You've still got some of his face under your fingernails," Nine says to Eleven with more than a little disdain.

Eleven checks, hides his fingers by folding his arms as he grumbles, seen.

"You're just jealous," he responds to the old man.

"Of what?!"

"Please! Can we just—" Two pleads, more with annoyance than anything else.

"He's right. Just start it up already," Six moans.

As Eleven reaches out to search for the "on" button on the figure, it comes to startling life without a single whir or creak. It moves its head to stare directly at Eleven.

"Lightning round transactional analysis. Your ego state will be evaluated. Those with the least offensive social track records will be spared until there are only two of you."

The female android speaks in a shockingly calm, anchored voice without a single sign of biological restraints. Like a voice wafting through the air yet not losing any of its potency mid-breeze.

"What the hell happened to morality roulette?" Two blurts out.

They mull that over in their heads for a long moment.

"Well, shit. Which one of us goes first?" Six asks.

"Transactional what the fuck? I don't even know what half of that means," Nine snorts.

"Quelle surprise, asshole," Eleven deadpans at Nine.

"You. You go, Nine," Two says with a snap of his fingers.

Nine glances back at the android, who just waits intently for someone to volunteer. Her stare is unnerving and utterly interminable.

"Can't be worse than Breakfast Melee, right?" Nine chuckles, fidgeting with his blood-caked hands.

No one matches his nervous amusement. Six, Two, and Eleven just stare at him, dead-eyed.

Nine looks as if he's about to fill the awkward silence again but the android's emotionless voice intercepts him.

"Juror Eleven. You once said about our fearless presidential leader that "he was a cocksucking pigfucker" and "if I had better aim, he'd be a dead man.""

There's no invidious or spiteful tone to her voice at all. Even the demeanor of a physician nearing retirement reading test results to a frequent patient would be an exaggeration of emotion.

Eleven balks; completely caught off guard.

"Wait. Wait a minute. I deleted that post! I'm a pacifist!"

With lightning speed, the android leaps from her seat and tackles Eleven to the floor, wrapping its hands around his throat and squeezing with inhuman strength. Everyone else flinches at the alarming rate at which things have escalated, but don't dare interfere.

Eleven gags and wretches and gurgles and soon, with a few pops and cracks and squishes, the android has strangled him completely to his death and ripped out his larynx and Adam's apple, tossing them to the floor with a sad, muffled flop. No heavy breathing, no heaving chest. Just quiet equilibrium. She returns to her seat and adjusts her suit jacket with a pair of wet red hands.

After an interminable silence, Two is the one who speaks first.

"Who would say something like that? I mean, seriously. God damn fascists."

"You're next, Nine. Thrill me," Six says with impatience.

"Says who? You in charge now? Last time I checked, the foreman left the building a while ago, so to speak. If we're going by numbers, Two's the boss now."

"Forewoman, Nine. Forewoman," Six almost sneers.

"Foreperson. Don't assume anything. Jesus," says Two as he practically cuts her off.

"Age before beauty, boomer," Six says as she bobs her head from side to side, trying to get Two back on her wavelength. He does with a reluctant smile.

Nine harrumphs.

"Fine. I'll pass this one with flying colors. Some of you all need to think before you put all your shit out there for everyone to see."

"Juror Nine. You once posted that "LGBTQIA should be changed to SFAQNTD" which you claimed stood for "Stupid Fags And Queers Need To Die.""

Nine goes white. Stammers.

"...I--I was a kid when I said that. I didn't mean it. I'm gay! I'm—"

He backs up, toward the far corner of the room, seemingly trying to escape from the withering yet non-judgmental gaze of the android in the smart pantsuit with the bloody hands. None of it matters because the android leaps from her chair again and closes a frighteningly long distance to pounce on Nine, who screams the squeal of an animal pinned down by a vicious predator and knows it's about to die.

"Help me! Help m—"

No help comes from Six or Two. What kind of help could they offer?

"Would have loved to record this for my StarFace account," Six declares, quietly crestfallen at the missed opportunity.

"Same," Two says with the same level of disappointment.

The android delicately pulls Nine's spine from his body, along with his skull attached to it. It was kind enough to leave his pelvis in what's left of his body. The brain is still encased in Nine's skull until the android swings the spine/skull combo like a mace against the wall and shatters the bone, letting most of the brain splat to the floor after sliding down the wall in a soupy mess, leaving a goop trail all the while.

"Jesus. Didn't see that one coming. SFAQNTD? It's not even a clever acronym." Six says.

"Are you saying you support his homophobia?" Two asks, indignant.

"He said he was gay!"

"You can't even answer the question. Do you even hear yourself?"

Six eyes a butter knife in between her and Two. Two sees it as well.

The female android adjusts her pantsuit once more and looks directly at Two and Six at the same time, one eye on each Juror. It makes Two gasp and Six move back in her seat.

"Lightning round transactional analysis has concluded. Juror Eleven was deemed to suffer from Parent Ego State and Juror Nine from Adult Ego State. Thank you for your cooperation."

The android also spots the knife and keys in on it with both eyeballs.

"You may now proceed with the final selections process."

As the android leaves the room with a methodical clump-clomp of her heels, Six and Two don't need to be told twice to reach for the knife.

And that's exactly what they both do.

*   *   *

Later in that whirlwind of a day, in that same courthouse, in the bustling, buzzy courtroom, Juror Two sits in the middle of an empty jury box. Blood still caked on his face and clothes. A wide smile ear-to-ear.

The stern judge with a stern, bristle brush mustache and a stern smoker's cough who might as well be named Judge Sternwell Sterns presides over the day's events. The stenographer is the female android from before, blood still all over her clothes and frame. Blood-dried hands type away furiously whenever anyone speaks.

A holographic crawl ensconced between the ceiling and the wall all around the room slowly and calmly states:

"**ANY OUTBURSTS OF EMOTION WILL BE PERCEIVED AS TOXIC AND MANIPULATIVE. PLEASE REFRAIN FROM EXPOSING YOUR PERSONAL FEELINGS TO OTHERS IN ATTENDANCE. THIS WILL BE PERCEIVED AS INFLICTING YOUR PRIVILEGE INVOL-UNTARILY ON YOUR FELLOW PERSON AND PUNISHABLE BY THE REVOKING OF YOUR SOCIAL MEDIA RIGHTS IN ACCORDANCE WITH THE "EVERYONE IS A STAR" ACT OF 2047. THANK YOU AND HAVE A DAY THAT SUITS YOU BEST FOR YOUR CURRENT PSYCHOLOGICAL STATE."**

And now the main event. The judge eyes Two with nothing but stern eyes and a stone-cold voice.

"...And on seventy-eight counts of first-degree murder, sixty-two counts of child abduction, twenty-three counts of rape of a minor, how do you the jury find the defendant...?"

Two stands, his proud smile refusing to abate.

"Your Honor, I the jury find the defendant not guilty by reason of emotional distress and seasonal affective disorder."

And there you have it. Enjoy the future, kids. It's coming up right behind you. You earned it. We *all* earned it fair and square. I ain't sticking around for this shit. Now where did I put that pesky gun? Son of a bitch. Always in the last place you look.

NOTES

I think this one is rather self-explanatory. More than any actual real-life parallels, I was more interested in paying tribute to Paul Verhoeven films and dystopian sci-fi fiction with a streak of jet-black humor. The thought of a near-future government or society determined to be as socially responsible as possible to the point of violent over-correction intrigues me to no end. Basically, our government would be like Jim Wynorski's *Chopping Mall* if it ever tried to clean up its act. The collateral damage would be monumental in the pursuit of perceived social justice. There's a huge difference between just being a good person and going about it every day as if no one is watching you and then on the other hand making sure everyone sees you attempting to be a good person when we all know what the truth really is. You aren't fucking fooling anyone.

THE FOURTH WHEEL

It's mid-afternoon in a quaint, middle-America kind of neighborhood. You know the one. Suburbs all the way. Secrets everywhere. There may or may not be a slight breeze wafting through the inoffensive decor of the cookie-cutter homes lining this particular cul-de-sac.

Marvin Sheffield and Earl Forbes are outside their buddy Derek Smallwood's house, waiting for the third man to kick start their night of semi-debauched drunkery and tomfoolery.

Marvin's the fast-talking, ill-tempered asshat of the crew and he wields this power like a toxic battle-axe of shitheadery. Earl, on the other hand, is the gullible fop of the trio. Always listening, barely registering anything. He has a permanent half-grin of the perpetually ignorant; blissful or not.

"...So, I said I'm not paying for that penguin unless you put those tacos back in your ass. That was the deal," Marvin bemoans to Earl.

"Then what'd he do?"

"He put 'em back in. Couldn't afford to keep the penguin."

"Unbelievable."

"I know, right? It's like he—"

Just then, Derek emerges from with his abode, trots down the front steps and heads toward the conversation of the century.

"Hey, bro. You finally escape the clutches of—"

"Don't say it!"

"Well, did you?"

"Yes. I'm good for the night. She's gonna go out, too. We'll have the place to ourselves for a little after the out-and-about portion of the evening."

"My man!" Earl goes for a high five, but Derek pretends he doesn't see it.

"So what *is* the plan my plan?" Derek asks Marvin as he rubs his hands together with a big smile.

"Do we need one?" Marvin smiles back even bigger.

"Utter chaos. I like it! Hope you pussies got your drinking hats on."

"Forgot my hat," Earl admits.

"Shut the fuck up, Earl." Marvin smacks him in the back of the head.

"Well, let's do this!"

They all make for Marvin's vintage 1999 Honda Civic hugging the curb nearby. Faded plum with chrome rims.

"Shotgun!" Earl squeaks at the other two.

Derek immediately punches him in the balls and pushes him out of the way. Earl staggers the other way in agony.

"Not in this lifetime, retard!"

As Derek goes for his hard-won shotgun seat, he scrunches up his face in mental agony.

"Shit! Almost forgot something, boys."

Derek changes course abruptly and heads for his car, parked at the lip of the cul-de-sac for some reason, about a hundred yards away from them.

"What the fuck, bro?" Marvin throws his hands up in impatience and confusion.

"I forgot something in my car. Be right back," Derek shouts as he presses forward to said car. A beige Toyota Tercel. Mid-2000s-ish.

The other two stare at him, befuddled, for barely a moment before turning back to each other for some hot take chit-chat. Derek gets smaller and smaller the closer he gets to his car as they ramp up their convo.

"Whatever the fuck that's all about," Derek grumbles.

"I know, right?"

"Ya gotta work on your witty repartee, man. It *fucking* sucks."

"Does it? I was practicing on my mom the other night."

"Is that all you were practicing?"

"What do you mean... Oh, man dude that's inappropriate. I mean—"

As the chatter goes absolutely nowhere, Derek is at his car and opens up the back passenger door, gesturing wildly at someone or something in the backseat. After a long moment, he coaxes a huge man boy out of the car. He's tall and wide; a monstrous, twentysomething Baby Huey.

Marvin and Earl don't see them yet as Derek gently pulls the giant young fellow down the street towards them.

"...That's not the point. See? A quick joke is like a quick jab. Bam! Right to the face. You never knew what hit you. Try it on me. I'll start up a conversation and you make an inappropriate joke out of the innocent recounting of my day. Got it?"

Marvin lays it all out to Earl like he was an exceptionally stupid pre-teen. Which he *was* on certain days.

"Okay, but what—"

Marvin and Earl finally spot Derek and his mammoth companion just as they're almost on top of them. They step back more than a few paces as they see the huge man-child. A permanent, crooked smirk-frown on his doughy face. His pants pulled up high and tight and his one-size-too-small t-shirt says **"SOMETHING"** in bold dark letters right across his chest.

"...the fuck...?" Earl beats Marvin to the punch on the involuntary reaction.

"Tact, Earl. Tact!" Marvin whispers to Earl before changing his tone to a much more welcoming one. "And who is this dandy gentleman we have here? Say, is that Drakkar Noir I detect on your person?"

Huge dude's expression never changes. He just stares off into the middle distance like someone was there, looking back at him just as stupidly.

"I told you; I left Something in the car," Derek explains yet again.

"I know you did. What's his name?" Marvin demands gently. He looks up again at the big guy and asks, "What's your name, bro?"

Nada. Just that blank stare in spades.

"He doesn't talk much. My wife's cousin."

"What's his name?!" Earl shouts, startling everyone but the massive guest.

"Inside voice outside, hm?" Marvin nudges Earl with a medium-strength elbow.

"Sorry."

"Something."

"Yes? What?"

"That's his name. Something."

"Come again?"

"He's, uh, special needs I think. But he's a good guy."

"You don't have to qualify that. He's standing right here."

"That was the catch for me going out tonight. He's gotta come with."

"Fuck that shit!" Earl bellows. "How's that for witty repartee?" He asks Marvin.

Marvin sighs and puts a patronizing arm around Earl.

"We'll try again later. After drinks." He smiles trim and quick at Derek. "Well, I guess we got a full car now. Four wheels all the way!"

Before they can all mosey, Derek sidles up to Marvin and half-whispers "Whatever you do, don't pay him *any* compliments. He *hates* them."

"...What the fuck?"

"Just trust me. We can party down with him as long as we don't say anything flattering to him. You got it?" Derek almost whispers.

"So, then what do we say to him? Tell him to go fuck his mother?" Earl whispers hoarse and loud right next to Something, who doesn't bat an eye. He isn't even swaying in position. A statue of ominous proportions.

"That one was actually pretty good, Earl. Now quit while you're ahead."

"Got it."

"We all good?" Derek asks, ready to hit the drinking bricks.

"Yup," Earl beams.

"Guess so," Marvin sighs.

Something is good to go, too. At least, they assume so. They all look at him for any sign of life. For longer than a few seconds.

"Awesome. Boys' night out!" Derek yelps as he jumps up in the air, fists clenched like he's expecting a retro freeze frame.

"Party down, bitches," Marvin agrees as he bobs his head.

"Yay!" Is all Earl can add.

* * *

Their watering hole of choice for the evening is the same fucking place they always end up at. Molly's Trough. An abyss-in-the-wall imbibery with all the fixings: a drunk regular passed out at the bar, a sassy brassy bartender in her mid-forties with a quick quip for everyone within earshot, a robo-jukebox that only seems to play "Freebird" and "The Cha-Cha Slide" and of course, a pool table complete with two jock townies who can't stop staring at the bartender's tits. Ah, the bar life. Nothing like it.

There's only a few other patrons dotting the premises, getting their alcohol on in various ways and means. Oh, and our intrepid trio and their new companion, a Mr. Something.

While Derek, Marvin, and Earl sidle up to the bar proper and order some shots, Something plants himself at a table in the back corner of the bar. Near the bathrooms. Leering wide-eyed at any passersby.

"Special needs, huh?" Marvin says to Derek, more than a little sarcastically.

"He'll warm up eventually. Just start drinking. And *don't* compliment him."

"Can I call him a cunt?" Earl asks, eager as a beaver.

"Sure, buddy. Sure." Derek pats him on the back hard as he downs a shot of tequila.

Soon, one shot becomes two and two becomes more and the night unfolds into a blackout blur of liver damage and poor decisions. Something has gone from the back corner table to the back side table, near the window. Staring out of it as if someone was out there calling to him.

Marvin finds a girl who's half-interested in him and hits on her like she's fully interested. Derek and Earl attempt to play darts on the ramshackle dart board that looks like it was a prop in *Road House*. The wall gets a good taste of their aim but the board itself remains untouched. Through it all, Something moves closer. To the pool table of all things, uncomfortably close to the townie hustlers cracking and racking to beat the band. They barely pay him any attention. Then, he's by the jukebox, staring at the bartender like they know each other. They don't. Or do they?

As Earl cha-cha slides around the room, Marvin and Derek commiserate at the bar, getting a closer look at Molly's tits than you can at the pool table.

"So what's with the guy? He doesn't seem special needs. Just like, socially awkward? The fuck is the real deal?"

"Look, I don't know for sure, but Laurie says whatever we do, don't pay him a compliment. He apparently can't handle it and it'll ruin our fucking night."

"Like he's gonna start crying or some shit? Was he abused as a kid or what?"

"I don't know man, I never seen it up close, but she says just don't do it and I trust her right there at that. She gave me the weirdest look when she said it. Like it kinda creeped me out."

"Dude, are we in any danger right now? Be straight up with me."

"Nah, I don't think so. We just gotta take good care of him."

"But just don't be nice to him. Makes a lot of fucking sense. Jesus."

"I didn't say that, just don't compliment him. That's all. Anything else is business as usual my man."

Derek lifts his whisky glass to cheers with Marvin, who reluctantly meets him with his own highball.

"Chin chin, bro," Derek says with a grin.

Marvin starts to drink but stops mid-sip. Takes his glass away from his now-pursed lips.

"But you said he was a good guy earlier. He was right there. Not a god damn thing happened."

"I said it to *you* guys. Not to him. That's the key. Don't tell him directly and I think everything's fine. Word?"

"Yeah, I guess. Word." Marvin resumes his drink action.

Earl cha-cha slides up to the jukebox, and by proxy Something, and selects Christopher Cross. Something doesn't seem to care either way as Earl tries to dance with him. "Tries" being the operative word. He just bumps into him a few times like they were passing shoppers at a crowded department store.

"You're a terrible fucking dancer!" Earl shouts over *"Saiiiiilllllliiiiing takes me awayyyyy…"*

Without any preamble, Something bursts into uproarious laughter, thick spittle landing atop Earl's head.

"Good one, Earl!" Derek shouts over to him.

"Keep it up, smoothie!" Marvin adds.

Something's eyes shift to the shot of tequila in Marvin's hand.

Marvin sees it and smiles mischievously.

"You want in on this, bro?"

Something moves closer. It's as if he glides, impossible as it sounds. If you try to look directly at his legs, something else distracts you from it. Something ethereal? Or maybe it's just the jukebox. Now Earl has chosen "Eye in the Sky" by The Alan Parsons Project. He insists it helps the tequila go through smooth.

As Something closes the distance between himself and Marvin, he reaches for the shot glass, still filled with off-brand liquor store cactus hooch disguised as the good stuff. With one stiff motion, the big guy whips it out of Marvin's hand and downs it. After a moment, he just nods.

Everyone in the bar cheers and hoots and hollers, the weirdo has eased the tension and become one of them for now.

More shots are ordered all around and the night descends ever further into inebriation and unreliability.

*   *   *

Back in Derek's neighborhood, anyone with any sense of responsibility is fast asleep or at least minding their own business with as little light or noise as possible.

Inside Derek's abode, however, the order of the hour is loud and unfiltered.

Derek, Marvin, Earl, and Something are on a beat-up, old puke-green couch in the basement, still drinking heavily. They've switched from tequila shots to Guinness. *In the clear*.

Earl insists on playing late 70s and early 80s soft rock on his phone, connected to Derek's purple, pill-shaped Bluetooth speaker, only because Derek is too drunk to object.

"Yacht rock?" Earl thinks out loud.

"Hot rock? How's that?" Derek yells over "Captain of Her Heart."

"Ya-gh-tttt rock!" Marvin scream-enunciates.

"Fucking what?" Derek grows angrier the more confused he gets.

"Yacht rock! That's what it is," Marvin elbows Derek with a chuckle.

"Cock rock. More like it," Derek mumbles.

"It prevents bar fights. Scientifically proven," Marvin says, more than a little proud of his useless trivia knowledge.

"I think you mean it causes 'em," Earl butts back in.

"Nah. It prevents them. I seen it in action."

"Will you shut the fuck up about the fucking yacht rock. Jesus Fuck Christ," Derek finally intervenes, barely able to form syllables properly.

All three of their speaking abilities are now nothing more than a slurring salad of shitfaced. Earl just a little more understandable than the other two.

"I can't believe Molly didn't want to come back with us."

"I can. Look at us. Would *you* come home with us?"

"Uh, yeah. Of course I would. I'm me."

"That's cuz you're easy, Marv."

"Shut the fuck up, Earl. You work on your witty repartee yet? The jukebox scenario don't count. Gotta be consistent and shit."

"Actually, yeah."

Both Derek and Marvin do an exaggerated double take. Genuinely surprised, though. Their body language exaggerated by the sheer volume of alcohol coursing through their veins.

"Okay, let's hear it," Marvin demands.

"Wait. Use it on Something. I wanna hear this again."

They all go quiet and just look to Something, who has been quietly drinking and smiling at the three the whole time. Nothing more, nothing less.

"You sure? I mean…" Marvin looks back and forth between Derek and Something, hoping Derek picks up on his intent of nonverbally insinuating Something is still not to be fully trusted.

"Yeah, like he's a total—"

Earl gives the universal signal for a crazy person, the swirling finger next to the head.

"It's fine, bro."

Derek nods at Something and winks. Something remains as he is, no acknowledgement of anything transpiring.

"Hey, bro," Derek says to Something.

Something shifts his head to lock on to Derek's eyes, the rest of his body not moving at all.

"Earl's got something to say to you."

Something signals he's all ears by not responding at all.

"Uh… So, like what's your mom think about you having no dick?"

Something just shrugs instinctively.

"'Cuz when I asked her, she said "what dick? I thought that was my daughter!"

Everyone laughs at the average joke mostly out of intoxication. Except for Something. They notice he's not laughing along with them, and they stop abruptly. Then, after an agonizingly long moment, Something laughs so hard it seems as if his guts are about to eject from his esophagus at any traumatizing moment. A deep, bassy belly laugh that startles all three guys. His laugh lasts for minutes as the guys just stare on in incredulity, like they're locked in a time and space vacuum and the rest of reality has simply ceased to exist. When Something finally avails himself of all his laughter, he gives Earl a solid, meaty thumbs up, which looks like he manicures said thumb with his teeth.

"Holy shit, he likes it!" Derek shouts involuntarily.

"Nice work, Earl," Marvin gushes as he pats his buddy on the back.

Earl gets up, laughing all over again and heads over to Something for a quick fist bump, which he gets, causing him to grin like an excited toddler.

"Hey thanks man, you're a really great guy!"

A switch flips inside Something's brain.

"...*You're a realllly grrrreaaatttt guyyyy....*" Something bellows deep down in his intestines.

His eyes bulge wildly, and his mouth opens wide like a pod person from a Body Snatchers movie. Preferably the one with Donald Sutherland.

"Oh shit, Earl you fucking dumb son of a—" Derek realizes too late that there's probably no escape from whatever's about to happen.

"What the fuck—" Marvin's now on his wavelength too.

Something screams a decidedly inhuman scream and begins to shake and vibrate all over. He snatches Earl by the throat, rips his tongue out of his mouth, throws it in Marvin's lap and snaps Earl's neck like stale, brown celery. A sharp CRRRACK registers through Earl's neck meat and Something's ham hocks as a waterfall of blood gushes from Earl's mouth. Marvin freaks out at Earl's tongue in his lap, trying to bat it away with scared, shaking hands.

"Great! Really great! A great guy! Really!" Something booms through gritted teeth.

Earl's tongue lands in Derek's lap, who vomits without a word spoken.

"What the fuck?!" Marvin screams, ready to puke himself.

"I told you not to compliment him!"

"I thought he'd start crying or leave or something! Not fucking—"

Something lunges for Derek with a primal screech and bear hugs the shit out of him. The puke soon appears. Everywhere. All over Derek's purpling face, Something's chest and shoulders, the floor, you name it.

"Quick… You… Gotta… Insult him…"

Something crushes the life out of Derek, squeezing what's left inside him directly out of his mouth. Blood. Bile. Organs. The works.

"Jesus Christ!" Marvin hollers, turning to run and slipping in the puke and blood that is now a dominant feature of Derek's basement lounge. Something drops Derek's crooked husk to the floor and reaches for Marvin, now drenched in bodily fluids not his own.

"Hey man, your…your… Your mom, she's like so fucking—"

Something is too quick to even care about Marvin's attempted insult and punches his teeth down his throat. He then lifts Marvin with both hands, while Marvin gags and chokes on his own teeth, and breaks his spine in half over his knee.

"Really…great…guy! Hey man! You are! Great guy, really! A REALLY GREAT GUY!!!!!!" Something warbles, drenched in the blood and puke of his former drinking buddies.

* * *

The security light on Derek's back porch shines down onto Something digging three deep graves, side by side. A dog barks from a neighbor several houses down. Pure silence besides the errant canine and Something's methodical SHUNK-CHINK shovel stabbing as he finishes the resting places of Derek, Marvin, and Earl.

Speaking of the three, they've been placed neatly next to each other, discreetly covered with bedsheets procured from the upstairs linen closet. Something chose a nice spring floral pattern for Derek, art deco downhill skiers on electric blue for Marvin, and a sensible pink, purple, and white plaid pattern for Earl. Something's come down considerably from his kill rage and merely mumbles now, occasionally raising his voice to just above a moan or a groan.

"You're a really great guy. Great guy! Really great! You are. You're great. A really great guy! Guy! Great! Really a great really guy are you? You are! Great guy!"

Rambling on and on, he finishes the depth of the graves and slides each guy gingerly into their respective corpse holes, sheet still firmly on them. He fills the holes with alarming speed and tamps the dirt piles down hard with the shovel. Hard but caring.

"Really great guy!"

* * *

Back inside Derek's house, Something has found the shower and stands in a stream of scalding hot water, fully clothed, head down, still mumbling. Blood, dirt, and puke comes off in streams and chunks as he occasionally shakes his titanic frame side to side like a hairless mastiff on two legs.

"Great. Really great…"

* * *

In the open night air, where no dogs can be heard at all now, Something trudges back to Derek's car at the start of the cul-de-sac; soggy, squishy clothes leaving a huge wet snail's trail the whole way. His shoes squeak on the pavement, daring anything else to make noise this late. *This early?*

He awkwardly slides into the rear passenger side. After a moment of staring straight ahead, he pulls the passenger door shut. Neither loudly nor quietly. Just shut.

"…Great."

NOTES

This one was originally created as a short screenplay I intended to direct myself. I flirted with it for years and it was going to be the next short we made after *What's For Dinner?* That never happened and I submitted it to a few contests and film fests to see what shook loose. The closest it got to being made was when it placed at the Drunken Film Fest in the UK, and they wanted to option it to produce over there. I was excited at first, but after a while it just didn't seem right. These guys with English accents? I couldn't picture it. They also wanted me to make a few changes in the rewrite that I was not a fan of. *C'est la vie.* Now it's here in this collection where it belongs. It still might end up as a short film; I do already have the screenplay, after all. I enjoy writing dumb stories about dumb guys doing dumb things. You're not punching down and you can get away with pretty much anything. Whether or not anything here or in other stories like *What's For Dinner?* or *Late Submission* is autobiographical in any way is up to you, gentle reader. Come to think of it, these characters with English accents might be even funnier.

A ransacked bathroom.

The faucet runs furiously. The mirror cracked and smashed.

Perched on the toilet seat is a frightened young woman in her late twenties.

Lisa.

Her makeup smeared all over her face. Sobbing intermittently.

Her terrified eyes fixed on the locked door. The handle jostles violently. Someone trying to get inside. A series of fierce, loud bangs at the door.

She shudders and screams uncontrollably. The bangs stop abruptly and soon Lisa tries to calm her breathing. Still lightly sobbing, eyes never leaving the doorknob.

"Leave me the fuck alone!"

From the other side of the door comes a familiar voice...

"...Come on, Lisa. Let me in..."

It's Lisa's exact same voice. Reflected back at her. It pauses dreadfully. Then...

"...It's so dark out here..."

Lisa pulls out her phone, frantically trying to call someone. It rings and rings and rings. She curses, panicked and beyond frustrated.

The violent banging from the other side of the door returns and intensifies to an unbearable level as Lisa screams and scream and screams.

Then it stops again. And the door just creaks open. Wide. A terrified Lisa's eyes bug out, expecting to see something awful. But there's no one there. The hallway dark and empty. The only sounds are her heavy, frantic breathing.

"...Hello?"

Nothing...

*   *   *

Fog rolls in from the deep woods. A lonely, old, and cracked road stretches on forever in both directions. Will stands at the edge of the road, peering through the trees against the fading light. He's got his hands on his knees and pants as if he's just run a mile.

"...Hello?"

Nothing. Will is visibly frightened. Something is wrong here.

"Why are you following me?"

A slight rustle of leaves. Will squints to see where it came from. And then nothing.

"Answer me...!"

Silence. It unnerves Will to the point of near breakdown. And then he sees it. From behind a tree slinks a smirking, wide-eyed figure. Himself. Will backs away, trips over a log, and lands on his rear. Terrified. The thing that looks like himself waves briefly and then just continues to stare at Will. Just as the thing moves its mouth to speak...

Will wakes with wide eyes and a sharp breath. Splayed out on his couch. Safe in his home. He looks at the clock. Wipes his brow. Sweating? Strange. Looks around. Seems a little lost. Befuddled. Sees his cell phone on the floor. Checks it. Three missed calls. All from Lisa. He calls her back. Eyes darting nervously around the room. It's so very quiet. The phone rings and rings and rings. No answer. Will becomes even more nervous. It goes to voicemail.

"This is Lisa. Obviously."

106

And then the message BEEP.

"...Hey, it's me. Saw you called. Sorry. Had to close my eyes for a little bit. Ended up dozing pretty hard. Call me back when you get a chance. Something I want to talk to you about... Hope you're okay."

He hangs up. Rubs his face. Looks around his deathly quiet surroundings. Still clearly affected by the dream.

In his uncluttered kitchen, Will makes coffee. Sniffs it. Shuffles back to the living room.

As he sits back down, a loud pounding comes from down the hall.

BANG. BANG. BANG.

The front door? Will freezes for a moment. More pounding.

Will peeks around the corner, down the hallway leading to the front door.

BANG. BANG. BANG.

The pounding grows more and more frantic. Will creeps down the hallway, fearful of what's behind the door.

BANG. BANG. BANG.

He reaches the door and unlocks it. Hesitates before opening it. No more knocks come from the other side.

"...Hello?"

No one answers.

"...Is that you? Lisa?"

Nothing. He opens the door at a creak and standing there, still as a statue, is Lisa. She looks cold and pale. Just staring off into the distance. She looks soaking wet, but Will reaches out to touch her and she's bone dry.

"Hey. Did you get my call?"

No response. She just stares past Will and into the house.

"What's up? What's the—"

Will realizes something quickly.

"Did...did something happen to you? What is it?"

Still nothing.

"You can tell me."

She finally looks up at Will. But only with her eyes.

"It's alright. Come on in."

Will sits across the table from Lisa. Steaming cups of coffee for both of them. Will nurses his. Lisa hasn't touched hers. Just stares straight past Will, not a single part of her moving an inch.

"Look, I'm sorry about missing your calls earlier. They've been killing me at work lately and I needed the extra shuteye."

Will takes a sip of his coffee.

"Truce?"

Nothing from Lisa. Just that stare.

"Are you sure you're okay?"

Lisa's eyes shift from straight ahead to right on Will's face. It's unsettling but Will tries not to show his unease.

"...Was it something at work? Did Kevin make another pass at you? I swear that guy can't take a hint."

He tries a chuckle to defuse the tension. Still nothing from Lisa. An awkward, uncomfortable silence ensues. After what seems like an eternity:

"So, uh, I had that dream again. I mean, I guess it's a nightmare."

He stares down at his coffee, trying to avoid her awful gaze.

"It's not so much that it looks like me. It's more that I can't tell which one is actually me. What if I'm the one behind the tree?"

He looks back up at Lisa.

"Know what I mean?"

After another agonizing stretch of silence, Lisa finally speaks.

"It's for you."

Will freezes.

"What...?"

Will's phone rings. He flinches violently. Lisa remains still as a corpse. With a shaking hand, he answers it.

"...Hello? As the voice on the other end talks, Lisa's face twists into a smirk. Much like the one on the thing behind the tree in his dream. A frightened Will can barely pay attention to the droning voice while looking at her.

"...That's...that's not possible. She's right here. She's not... I'm telling you she's sitting right here! What?! That's not... I don't—"

Will lowers the phone from his ear with a shaky hand. Just staring agog at the grinning Lisa.

"Who are you?" He demands, trying to shore up what little courage he has. "What are you?"

Will backs slowly toward the kitchen, never unlocking eyes with Lisa. With a sudden jerk of speed, he breaks eye contact and dashes into the kitchen.

Will hurtles toward the countertop, almost smashing into it. He flings open a drawer and plunges a hand inside before quickly pulling out a large kitchen knife. He looks back toward the living room with a sweaty brow of terror and confusion.

Re-entering the living room in a barely controlled panic, Will holds the knife straight out, pointing it all around the room in short-breathed hysteria. Eyes wide and full of fear. Lisa is gone. Nowhere to be seen.

Will rushes into the hallway, looking all around for Lisa, making his way to the front door.

Will clambers out onto his front porch, searching for signs of Lisa. Somewhere. Anywhere. Nothing. She's gone. Like she was never there to begin with.

*　*　*

Deep in a dense forest, paramedics and cops encircle the body of a woman lying face-down in the dirt, the centerpiece of a very bizarre crime scene. Or an accident scene. Hard to tell. Around the woman's neck is a noose with a length of rope cut off about two feet from her neck. In her clenched left hand is a shotgun. No expended shells in sight. Her bare feet are caked in mud and dirt. Her body faces outward from the deeper part of the forest, as if she came from there. But there are no footprints to be seen. Behind her are a pair of heavy men's boots, placed as if someone had followed her and then just jumped out of them and vanished without a trace. Shards of broken glass surround her body. A pool of blood seeps into the dirt from her concealed face, hidden in part by her matted head of hair.

A rosy-cheeked and moribund sheriff's deputy and a silver-haired, pockmarked detective stand around the scene, completely baffled and at a loss for words.

"Lift her head up."

A young, rookie coroner gently holds the corpse's head with two gloved hands and lifts her head up enough to see her bloody, mangled face. Eyes still wide open, locked in eternal fear. Forever staring at something in the middle distance.

Will lets out a guttural cry behind them. Drops to his knees. It's Lisa. No doubt about it.

The sheriff's deputy looks about to have a full-on conniption fit as he witnesses Will's breakdown.

"What the hell is he doing back here? Who let him in? Get him outta here!"

The detective winces. Makes a move for Will and puts a hand on his shoulder.

"It's all right. I called him."

Will looks shell-shocked. Out of body.

"I got your call..."

"Yeah, that's right. I'm so sorry you had to see this, but..."

"I got the call. She was right there. Listening. She was there."

"Oh jeez. We got a basket case. Get him outta here will ya?"

A state trooper and an EMT gingerly put their arms around Will and gently escort him away from the scene. As he goes with them, he spots someone in the woods with a sudden jerk of his head; ensconced in a thick clump of trees a good deal off in the distance. Someone watching him.

"Hey..."

Will tugs the trooper's coat sleeve urgently and points to the figure.

"Did you talk to *him* yet?"

"Who?"

And then, in that awful moment, Will realizes the figure in the tree line is him. Smirking. Waving.

The thing moves its mouth to speak.

Will screams.

NOTES

This one works best written as a nightmare scrawled down on paper immediately after waking up. I had a dream similar to this once and it freaked me out so bad I didn't want to go back to sleep the next night. As I said before, doppelgangers terrify me. I balk at clowns and dolls and all that other shit. The notion that somewhere out there is your exact copy and happens to be the harbinger of your doom chills me to the bone. I've got goose pimples right now just typing this. I don't like using the word auteur to describe a creative individual most times, but Japanese director Kiyoshi Kurosawa is a god damned auteur in every sense of the word. Films like *Pulse* (aka *Kairo*), *Cure*, *Doppelganger*, *Retribution*, and *Charisma* prove that beyond a shadow of a doubt. But the one that does it for me personally is the 2000 film *Séance* (based on the British book and movie *Séance on a Wet Afternoon*). It features the creepiest depictions of ghosts and doppelgangers I think I've ever seen in a movie, and I've watched a good chunk of them. What I'm trying to say is that these story notes are just excuses for me to recommend movies to you. I think that's admirable of me. Getting back to the point; doppelgangers, when done right, are unbelievably frightening and I'm not done exploring my main source of terror (besides the one about dying before my daughters form solid memories of me). Not by a long shot.

MICK WINKERSON'S AWFULLY BIG DAY

The gun feels at home in the breast pocket of my suit jacket. Like it's always been there.

I must admit, it feels nice that no one on set knows it's there. Fifteen years of not missing a show buys me some goodwill after all. No security checks, no questions.

"It's just Mick. He's good people."

I am *good people, godammit.*

What day is it? *Fuck.* Friday.

Friday shows are always the worst. End-of-the-week desperation infects the contestants. As if their default desperation weren't enough.

* * *

I'll never understand what drives these people. What spurs them on to take another crack at a shit sandwich that's already on loan to them and the interest increases with every bite. It was fun at first, all those years ago. Brave new world. Uncharted territory and all that. The networks were actually going to let us kill people on live television. We knew dummies would sign up in droves, we just had to get the go ahead from the people in charge.

And why shouldn't they say yes? Death was everywhere else anyways. Might as well trot it out onto primetime for every greedy, fame-obsessed idiot to gorge on.

That's where "What's My Sin?" came in.

And it came in like a frigging nuclear warhead at that.

Any sane, rational individual would listen to the rules and laugh. Walk away.

But sane, rational individuals were hard to come by these days. The world kept fucking over the common citizen so bad and so often that there was no coming back at that point. Their corporate masters had them hook, line, and sinker with no way out. Well, no way out except for two options.

Get filthy rich or drop dead.

Our show offered both.

Now you see the appeal, I wager.

So did I back then. Being the host with the most felt like my shot at the big time. My shot at getting rich. Rising above a writhing mass of the hopeless and the mindless.

It worked. For a while.

The rules? Oh, yes. The rules.

"What's My Sin?" is a deceptively simple game. It's designed to benefit the creators and the audience. The players are the last to be considered.

The crux of the show is the gun. Not your average, deafening bullet blaster. A state-of-the-art breakthrough in technology that can sense your worst deeds and thoughts.

The gun is used as the centerpiece of a live game of Russian roulette between four people from all walks of life. Well, most walks of life. The rich need not apply.

Everyone takes a turn putting said gun to their temple, injecting a tiny microchip that interacts with the gun in so many interesting ways. After that initial round, each player places the gun up to their temple once more and pulls the trigger. The gun, in concert with the microchip, senses the player's worst transgressions and beliefs and announces one at random for the whole nation to hear. The contestant with the worst sin or thought out of the lot has their head obliterated by a tiny plastic explosive in the microchip they willingly inserted into themselves earlier. The game continues until one player's left alive, earning them fifty million dollars.

Now, fifty million dollars might seem like Heaven *and* Earth to you, but for the conglomerated megacorps that rule America, fifty million is a half-day's earnings. We give that away five times a week for fifty-two weeks a year. For fifteen years now. It's an easy get-out-of-everything card for the average Joe or Jane, but just enough to blow in a lifetime if you're either really stupid or just plain careless. Or both. A lot of people are aggressively both. And that's what the megacorps counted on. Keep slaving away at that horseshit job you hate in hopes you'll end up on our show one day. It was worth the torment. Like I said, a literal Heaven on Earth. But even if you win, Hell is right around the corner for the careless. Then it's back to the bread line and your barely-above-minimum-wage warehouse job or working for tips delivering food to what's left of the upper middle class. And they're all abysmal tippers.

At first, there was resistance. Naturally, of course. But you would have thought we were weaponizing free speech the way the public freaked out on our premiere episode. Leave it to America to eventually normalize everything horrible, though. Barely weeks in, just as many people wanted on the show as those that denounced it. It was all anyone could talk about. Ever. It dominated social media from night one to today. Politicians love it dearly because they could literally murder their family on Thanksgiving, throw the bodies through the windows of their neighbor's house and piss on a troop of passing Girl Scouts before lighting them on fire and it would show up for about fifteen minutes in the daily news cycle then disappear amongst the fervor for "What's My Sin?" Three months elapsed and people were lining up to have their heads exploded and everyone else couldn't get enough of the show watching at home. Seasons? Fuck seasons. We were every weekday from January to December. There were no sweeps weeks for us. It was just one big god damn sweeps year, for fuck's sake.

And the people? Oh, the people! God bless them one and all. Especially the ones who think they have better lives after hearing about the sins of those on the show when their issues are just as bad. We didn't weaponize free speech. We weaponized *hypocrisy*. And it made us all filthy fucking rich.

Oh, and the viewers get to vote live on who dies every round. Fun for the whole family. Families *love* our show. Especially in the flyover states.

I know what you're thinking and yes, we *do* pay death benefits to the families of the losers. Fifty grand to each family. More than enough for funeral expenses and grief therapy sessions. We're not total monsters. The whole family has to sign a waiver for the contestant to be eligible. So don't fucking look at me like that, okay?

* * *

I look at the show format for today. Fucking Friday, as I said. Goddamn wild west on Fridays.

Who's on tonight? Let's see…

Clara Mann. Thirty-two. Single mother. Likes scrapbooking and dating. What a combo. Says here she'll do just about anything for her kids. Ha. No shit. Well, let's see if that's really true.

Malcolm Carver. Twenty-three. Damn. Another young fellow. Hope he's not another one of these crazy-ass protestors that commit a bunch of illegal and immoral shit and then come on the show to die in defiance of corporate greed. Yeah you really showed them. Fucking kids.

Esmerelda Seguero. Fifty-eight. Widow. Three kids. All grown up. Looks like another nothing-to-lose, everything-to-gain woman. They're dangerous. And crazy. Probably my pick.

Eddie Tran. Forty. Married. No kids. Mid-life crisis incoming, I bet. He's here because he either hates his wife or they're one missed payment away from debtor's prison. Tough break, my guy.

The look on *one* of their faces at the end of the night should be worth more than fifty million dollars. At least to me. For a few seconds, at least.

They're all on set, hanging about in their own way. Malcolm and Esmerelda are in their seats. Game faces on. Ready to go. Ready to die. Maybe. Eddie's hitting on Clara. Her "interested" face is remarkable. Or maybe she's into it. It doesn't really matter. Unless they've already fucked, that bullet train just left the station at top speed. Besides, there's no sex allowed on the show. That's a bridge too far and would get our asses cancelled. Tonight's fab four haven't spotted me just yet and I love that. I get to observe the rats before the maze starts.

"Thirty minutes, Mr. Winkerson."

The voice of my least favorite intern. Phillippe. A French dickhead going for a communications degree at Cornell. Even his whispering voice makes me nauseous. I won't miss him for a second.

"I know that. Are you trying to say I can't tell time?"

"Sorry, Mr. Winkerson."

"It's Mick. Now fuck off."

Phillippe flits off to do something vaguely French and annoying.

I guess the contestants heard all or part of that exchange because now they're looking at me.

Great. Here we go.

I stroll over to meet and greet them as I try to sense the gun up against my chest, nestled silently inside my jacket breast pocket. I'm anxious *and* excited for today's bonus round.

*   *   *

The show itself is a heinous blur. All I can think of is what I will say when it is time. How I will carry myself. These four schmendricks are the least of my concern. I'm on autopilot and make it look easy. Fifteen years of this shit and I'm ready to do it blindfolded. Also, I'm not the one repeatedly putting a delayed detonation trigger to my head.

After the chip round, Clara is up first. She scissored her kid's babysitter while the husband was smoking pot in her she-shed. The kid fell out of its bunk bed and cracked their skull while the shenanigans were occurring. Funny? Sure. Fucked up? Yeah. But the worst? Doubtful. Eddie purposely hit the brakes on a tailgater in traffic then sped off when the passenger flew through the windshield. Ouch. Esmerelda believed that Jews have telekinetic powers. She said so in a social media post from three years ago. Disturbing and weirdly specific to be sure. Malcolm punched his mom in the face once when she refused to let him go to a party at his girlfriend's house. Wow. That has to be it, right?

Well, America votes and decides Esmerelda is fucked, even though she had no followers to speak of to see her original post. Her screaming head disappears in a glorious nebula of red mist and plastique smoke. Color me shocked. I really thought she would make it further. Oh well. Malcolm and Eddie both get off lucky on that one, if you ask me.

Round two comes and goes and with it, Clara's head. Her sin is blaming a Black man for stealing her car when in actuality she just forgot where she had parked her cream-colored Lincoln Navigator at the mall one Saturday. The one with the license plate that says BLESSD1. Lazy racism. The public publicly hates that. Eddie made a dirty joke online once about clowns being bisexual or something and Malcolm stole his father's credit card to buy a hooker. An expensive one. At least he has class? Anyway, the top of Clara's skull almost hits the ceiling, which is quite the feat considering how high the clearance is in our new studio. I try to form some sort of joke in my head about blowing your stack and it almost makes me laugh. I got in trouble for that once.

Round three rears its ratings-grabbing head and proves to be a shocker. It's down to Eddie and Malcolm. I'm dead sure Eddie is winning all the marbles, but no. Not at all. America votes that Malcolm forcing his girlfriend to get an abortion is not as sinful as Eddie calling his mailman "colored." Oof. Eddie sounds like he's praying when the front of his face virtually teleports to the side wall while the rest of his skull just slides down his back and click-plops onto the floor.

Well, I can't say I'm not surprised at the outcome. I was Captain Incredulous when the show first started. Perpetually gobsmacked. The memes of my various reactions when someone's head exploded were an unkillable virus on the internet. Fifteen years wears away at you after a while, though. Nowadays I was just happy not to get any blood on me. My trademark tailored suits don't come cheap. And the dry-cleaning bills for them are the kind of nightmare stuff that twentieth-century genocides are made of.

"Congratulations! You just won big on What's My Sin!"

My voice is even more condescending than usual. Maybe I'm compensating for my impatience.

Malcolm looks like he just found Jesus sitting in his living room, just watching television. He jumps up and down, pumps his fist, screams wildly. Elated. Huh. I guess he's not one of those extreme protesters after all. Now *that's* a pity.

"Oh my God! Thank you, Mick. I love you. I love my life. Shout out to Mom and Dad. You're my everything. We're moving into a new house. We're each gonna get our *own* houses! Thank you God and Jesus for this blessing and please watch over the other contestants. May they rest in power."

Wow. I almost say the word audibly. Social media is probably all aglow with the fake love for this kid. Their veiled, faux-progressive racism. How he persevered. How they were glad a straight white guy didn't win. And I would agree with them. I'm all for fresh new faces. But it gets old, you know? I mean, change the record, guys. Am I right or am I right? It's all the usual lip-service playbook. I'm almost sorry I won't get to doom scroll on my phone after this one. But I know it'll be worth it. And that's enough this time.

Fuck it. Time to sign off.

I do my best Bob Barker as I place a gentle arm around the kid.

"You are one of my favorite winners in all of my fifteen years on this show, my dear Malcolm. It couldn't have happened to a better person."

Malcolm is all squeals and jumps; he expends his victorious energy like a joy fiend. I wish it's Eddie here next to me. Or Clara. Selfish fucks. Hell, even Esmerelda. This kid is *too* happy for what's about to transpire. Too hopeful. *How dare he?*

"As a surprise bonus, I have on the line the President of the United States of America just to talk to you. Let me grab the presidential phone, Malcolm."

The look of awe and raw emotion on this kid's face stops me for a second. I can't do this.

Then I remember. His sins. Just him being here. No decent soul belongs here. This is most definitely a place where angels refuse to tread. Or even mention.

I'm doing this kid a favor, godammit.

I continue to reach inside in my jacket breast pocket. I pull out the "phone" and paint the back of the show's set wall with Malcolm's brains and blood. He drops to the floor with the volume turned all the way down. Like a switched-off robot on spaghetti legs. No more merriment. No more excitement. Just peace and quiet.

I am jealous.

Without missing a single beat, I turn to the camera and flash my trademark, toothy Mick grin.

"Malcolm really showed you that American spirit, didn't he? He stuck it out and came out on top. What courage! You talk about the American Dream, folks. Well, right there is the very definition of the term. Just incredible."

I point to the floor of course. Where Malcolm is. Dreaming the American dream. I hope he appreciates what I've done for him. I know Clara or Eddie wouldn't.

Esmerelda *might* have. She *just* might have.

All cameras are still recording. I can faintly see one of the producers scurrying around in a huff. But they never try to cut the feed. And why would they? *This* is great television. This is what everyone wants. It's what they've *really* wanted all along.

I slide the gun into my mouth. I clench so hard I can't tell if I chip my teeth, or my teeth scratch the barrel.

I can now see the producers and cameramen out of the corner of my eye panicking. Waving their arms, sternly whisper-yelling at each other about what to do.

But the red light stays on, of course.

Say goodnight, Mick.

"And that's it for another episode of "What's My Sin?" Tune in next week so see which corporate fuck-puppet they replace me with. Goodnight, America. Burn in Hell!"

I glance at the headless losers slumped over onto the game table. Their blood converges together right in the middle. One giant melting pot. More like a wading pool. It's kind of beautiful.

I pull the trigger. At least, I think I do. The vibrations I feel and hear are not in fact my head exploding. It's my phone.

Of course. What timing. Someone calling to say don't do it. It's not worth it. All that shit.

Too late. I squeeze the trigger a smidge. The hammer cocks back a hair. So close now. These fucks can all watch what I think of the good life.

I happen to catch one of the producers frantically make the phone sign with his thumb and pinky. And then point upwards with another shaky finger.

The higher ups? Contract negotiations? Finally?

I pull my persistent phone out of my pocket with my free hand. I don't take the gun out of my mouth for a second. Forward momentum is precious in a situation such as this.

I answer with a surprisingly confident tone. Not at all what my inner voice sounds like right now.

"Go for Mick," I say with a muffled mouth full of gun.

As soon as the voice on the other end starts talking, I know exactly what I have to do.

And so I turn to the camera, smiling as best I can with a loaded gun in my mouth.

NOTES

What would happen if Richard Dawson's character Damon Killian from *The Running Man* survived that movie and just kept doing that gameshow for years to come? I feel like it would probably play out something like this in the end. Originally published in early 2021 in D&T Publishing's anthology *It's All Fun and Games Until Somebody Dies*, this story's lack of subtlety is absolutely intentional. As a film fest runner, filmmaker, and writer, being on social media is a necessary evil. One that takes a toll on me every single day. The utter indecency of humans is on display every second of every minute and it's doing more harm than good, no matter what your internet friends say. Add to that primetime network television and the curse of reality show programming (two things I've never been able to wrap my head around) and you have the perfect storm of American decadence and dumbfuckery. Humans are awful, terrible creations. No amount of goodwill or charity will ever make me change my mind. Every positive action from a group of humans is a direct response to a myriad of negative actions from the same species in a vain attempt to balance the equation. It's hardly ever the other way around. Think about that shit. Anyway, tuck in for the finale.

I'D HIT THAT

I had grown quite tired of masturbation. It held no amount of joy for me anymore. With the various and myriad genres of pornography exhausted ad infinitum, my listlessness grew monstrous. Fleshlights, sex dolls, anal stimulants; nothing helped. The drudgery of dating another human being in the hopes they would get it up and keep it up for me proved even more exhausting. I was at my wit's end. And my cock's, too. The poor, sore fella had had enough of the mundanity as well.

And then one day, when I was near the end, and I mean *the end*, I stumbled upon something so stupid, so ill-advised, that I simply had to try it.

I could just clone myself.

Why the hell hadn't I thought of that sooner?

I'll tell you why. Because it's dangerous as all hell. FDA approved for a little while now, sure. But sketchier than a pencil drawing of a back-alley mugging. The government implemented it to create a standing army in a pinch, but soon abandoned it after realizing (and witnessing) the countless things that could go wrong with a rushed batch. And with the original subject. Now any "licensed" mom and pop biotech startup could advertise clone batches thanks to the FDA cleaning up their unpredictability after a healthy corporate bribe and some overdramatic public grandstanding in front of the Senate.

But I had it all planned out. I felt so clever, like no one had ever thought of such a thing before. I was going to get one to do the cleaning, one to do the cooking, one to run the errands, one to go to work, and one to fuck.

It really sounded like a good plan at the time. That's how it all starts, you know. Sounds of plans and the like.

And then they *all* just wanted to fuck. Us. Ourselves. Nothing else got done.

God damn fucking clones. Literally.

The AuctionBlock ad couldn't have been clearer…

Clone batch for all your crucial needs. All we require is your body for unapproved clinical trials and you get your very own cadre of replicants. No credit check necessary.

That's it. Donate your body to science and get cloned for your efforts.

Now, I know what you're thinking. *Hey, back the fuck up. The fuck did you say? One to fuck? What?*

Oh come on, stop it. You've thought about it, too. I know you have.

Who knows what turns you on better than *you*? Right? Yeah.

Look, I didn't want it to end this way. Prying horny versions of me off my actual ass with a crowbar. Or a baseball bat. Or a hacksaw.

One time I had to use a blowtorch.

No, not down there.

To his face.

Horndog fuckstick never knew what hit him.

I did, though. A mouthful of ignited butane. It melts tongues in a hurry. He was all gurgles and a stream of red tongue juice faster than you could say felch five times in a row.

You ever try throwing a hornier, less empathetic version of yourself down a flight of stairs while their dick (or strap-on) is in your ass? You would think a potential trip down said flight of stairs would shrivel a cock (or disappear a strap-on) but good. Nope. I think it actually made it harder.

That's definitely not one of *my* peccadillos. I think it has something to do with the fact that after they're "born" they all branch off into different behavior patterns and thought processes. At least that's the theory. You ever see that movie *Godsend*? Kinda like that but less terrible. Or just more terrible in a different way, I suppose. Yes, I know it was a book, too. But who reads anymore? These assholes certainly don't. Probably because I don't. Didn't.

I'm getting ahead of myself. Way ahead, it seems. Let's start somewhere more salient, shall we?

* * *

The trip to the lab was easy-peasy. United Genetics, Inc. on Hull Street. The shitty part. A simple transaction if there ever was one. They took blood, semen, hair, mucus, saliva, urine, and even a turd from me. They also poked and prodded me for a bit, but I think that was just for their own personal spank bank. Then, a few more injections later and I was standing in front of a genetic oven waiting for my clones to bake. It was weird but also kinda soothing. Like watching blood-and-shit-filled Shrinky Dinks get big and hairy. And noisy. The screaming as they formed was not something I had anticipated. Took about six hours all told. I got tired of staring at the window and took a nap for the last half. Had to keep my stamina up for what was to come.

I'd like to say the car ride home was interesting, but unless your idea of interesting is five versions of yourself staring at each other waiting for the first one to break the ice, then it was most certainly not. I rented a minivan in preparation for such an occasion. The associate at the front desk of the rental office asked if it was for a family vacation. I told her if a vehicle to retrieve my duplicate sex slaves was a family vacation, then yes. Her nervous laughter triggered my gag reflex and I nearly vomited right then and there.

Once home, I set about the confusing and infuriating task of naming my clones. What's in a name, other than a Pavlovian method of immediate recall?

First thing was first before the names, though. They were all wearing the same outfit that I also happened to be wearing that day. The lab's sense of humor shining through. A plain tan t-shirt, left over from my days in the Air Force. Faded green cargo shorts I bought at a discount clothing store years ago. Black ankle socks, as anything higher than that gave me panic attacks. Old, squeaky sneakers that used to be bright orange but now just looked like rotten feet tangerines. No one ever mistook me for an undercover agent of the Fashion Police and that's the way I liked it.

I trudged over to the far end of the first floor to my recently inherited family home and made for the bedroom. I'm not going to get into the whole song and dance of how my parents died right now. Just know it was sudden. And inconvenient.

Ah, *my* bedroom. I hated stairs so I had made my father's old office my sleeping quarters. The upstairs had become a forgotten realm of sad memories and nostalgia. Once in my room, I stared in proud wonder at reams and reams of unfolded clean clothes mingled with dirty clothes worn several times in a row until the smell was noticeable even to me. That was my cutoff, apparently.

What to wear? I rummaged through the landfill of vestments until I found five suitable outfits for my new houseguests. I could hear them conversing amongst each other just outside my room. Chittering. Mumbling. Whispering. Were they already judging me so soon? Of course they were. I was a judgmental asshole above all else. Snickering about my wardrobe, guffawing at the lack of furniture in my abode. Whatever it was about, I knew I didn't like it.

I assigned each one of me a set of clothes distinguishable enough from each other that I could tell them apart upon sight. I hoped they would see the logic of my intentions and follow suit. Nothing was said initially, but I knew at least a few of them were silently figuring out how to fuck with me in this department.

Leroy was first. Yes, Leroy. A pair of my khaki slacks and a purple polo shirt helped me keep him straight from the others. Purple Leroy.

Bannister was next. It's a good name. A memorable name. I sure as hell wasn't planning on calling them Tom, Dick, Harry, Steve, and Joe. That was a recipe for mediocrity and disaster all at once. I'd sworn myself off from ever having kids, so this was the next best thing I suppose. Make every name count.

Anyway, Bannister was the recipient of my plaid board shorts and a Silver Moon Drive-In & Swap Meet t-shirt I bought in Lakeland, Florida one hot, muggy summer what now seems like ages ago. It was bright red. Red Bannister. Number two squared away and ready to go.

Number three came to be known as Fillmore. I wasn't messing around. These needed to be immediate recall kinds of handles. Torn jeans and a powder blue and white button up short-sleeved bowling shirt. Jeans Fillmore.

They were looking better and better by the second. I could remember where I was when I first wore those outfits and when I last wore them. It was like looking at a 3-D memory of my past self. Almost. They all still looked like I did these days and not twenty years ago, when it was easier to get pretty much anyone into bed. It was going to be hard to decide which one would be my designated fuck buddy and which ones were strictly work friends.

Nester, number four, obliged me by donning a black t-shirt with a picture of Roy Scheider reclining in a gravy ladle and the quote "You're gonna need a bigger boat." It went well with the camouflage cargo shorts I was able to find in the back of my musty, dusty closet. Nester Scheider. Done.

Lastly, Dresden sported a turquoise long-sleeve dress shirt with the sleeves rolled up and the only pair of jean shorts I've ever bought and yes, even the only pair of sandals I've ever owned. I hated ever showing my feet in public, but they didn't look half bad from this perspective. Weird.

Turquoise Dresden. And that made five.

And there you had it. Five Me's all in a row. Not exactly pretty maids or anything but I was sure one of them would do the trick for my particular needs.

Leroy. Bannister. Fillmore. Nester. Dresden. All dressed up with no place to go.

Done and done.

Now. How to choose?

Should I do it reality TV style and court each one, hoping they'll all develop their own personalities and I'll be able to clearly pick a winner? Hmm. That could cause infighting.

Maybe I should just do eenie meenie miney mo?

Sounded scientific enough.

So, I did.

And I ended up on Nester. Interesting. I was pot committed, no going back now. It wouldn't look professional at this point.

"Nester!" I said a little too loudly. It didn't startle him one bit, though. I mean, it didn't startle *me* one bit. Right? After all, I knew me already. In theory.

He gave a slight smile and shuffled over to me in my trademark way. Even if they were slowly developing their own branching personalities, thoughts, and memories, Nester looked and moved and smelled exactly like me. I was excited and terrified all at once. This was really going to happen.

First thing was first, though.

Assignments. Cleaning. Work. Cooking. Writing. Important tasks for important Me's.

Leroy was the designated work clone. Every day, eight to five without fail. To and from the office and nowhere else. At least for now. Don't want to complicate things so soon.

Bannister became the house chef. Three meals a day, six days a week. Saturday was a cheat day, and we could eat whatever we wanted. Most likely the vilest, greasiest takeout imaginable.

Fillmore was now housekeeper extraordinaire. Toilets scrubbed and lawns mowed. The works.

And Dresden was the gopher. Errands, social media, bill paying, all that jazz. It was an easy job. Tedious, sure, but probably the easiest of the four. I think he appreciated it. At least, that's the impression I got from his pronounced wink and smile.

That's what it meant, right? It couldn't possibly mean anything else. I remember doing that all the time to show my appreciation. Sure, it's been a while, but…

Tangents wouldn't do right now. I needed to remain focused. With their assignments divvied up, I got about the task at hand.

Fucking myself.

Thankfully, Nester seemed just as intrigued as I was at the prospect of 4-D masturbation. Or out-of-body masturbation. Why didn't I think of that? I guess I did, actually.

As the others puttered off to whatever I had assigned them to hold dear, I went about undressing Nester. He didn't seem to mind. In fact, the gentle touch of my fingers had already made him hard.

Wow. This should be easy.

Neither one of us had any idea of what to expect and just as I was wondering how to take the next step, he reached out and took off my own shirt. Just like that.

And voila, I was just as hard as he was. I was way more into this than I ever thought I would be.

Money well spent. Well, in theory, that is.

We didn't even have our pants off before we were sixty-nining each other through our zipper holes. Fast and furious sucking and stroking. We knew what rhythm and speed worked best for us without a word or even a bodily adjustment. It felt great. It felt amazing. It felt like…

Wait a minute…

When I sucked him off, I could feel it in my own dick.

What the fuck…?

How was that even possible?

He must have been feeling the same thing when I did it to him because when I did a double take at the sensation, so did he.

"Uh… You feel that?" I asked, wiping spittle from the corner of my mouth.

"…Yeah. Yeah, I feel that."

Without another word, he went back to fellating me with aplomb.

And so, I did as well. Who was I to turn my nose up at an added feature of this clone thing?

We both came in each other's mouths after a solid fifteen minutes or so of suck-moaning.

Glorious.

The funny thing was, I stayed hard.

And so did he. Even minutes after.

We kind of just laid there on the floor, on our sides, mouths still after-tasting of our own spunk, contemplating the fact that our rods remained.

A flicker in his eyes from my face to my cock, then back to my face signified he was cool with me fucking him in the ass.

So, I did.

For a long time. We took turns edging his own dick with his hand and then mine, keeping his load just under the surface of erupting.

I'd never been pegged much in the past, so our ass was still pretty tight in general. It was all I could do to keep from busting after only a few minutes. But I was really enjoying this out-of-body sex session so much that my mind kind of went to a place just outside of the room, like it was in voyeur mode, observing the two of us pumping efficiently, a sort of horny oil derrick. It kept me from losing the plot too soon.

After about thirty minutes of railing Nester Me, it was time to dump. It was the best orgasm I ever had in my life. Knowing I could blow my load in myself and have myself immediately detach from myself and then proceed to fuck me in the same fashion was weirdly satisfying. And just like with the sixty-nine session, I felt his dick in my ass in my own dick. I can't even describe the sensation properly without fucking it up. The closest thing I can relate it to is, well, a telekinetic handjob from a velvet fleshlight. Not that I've ever had that experience, per se, but I can imagine that shit rather well.

I think he (me) lasted a few minutes longer than I did, probably just to prove a point and have one over on me in that department. It sounded like something I would do to myself if given the opportunity. I've definitely done it to other people. In other departments, of course.

We lay there, spent, for at least an hour. Bodily fluids of more than one kind drying on us and the floor. No words were said. What do you say to *yourself* after a sexual mind meld that isn't redundant bullshit?

We did, however, jinx each other when we finally mused out loud what could be on the menu for dinner.

* * *

133

Dinner went well. Bannister made manicotti from scratch along with procuring a choice Merlot from the nearest Wine Knot store – an establishment that specialized in red wines and freshly made garlic knots. A specific niche to be sure, and one that was filled nicely based on their daily foot traffic. Conversation consisted mostly of mindless, automatic small talk amongst one another. Five lost souls cut from exactly the same cloth trying not to stare too long or too hard at one another for fear of being pegged a pervert, even though that's exactly what we were. Six if you count me. The original me.

After mastications and libations, we were at an impasse. What do we *do* with ourselves? I mean, I knew what Nester and I preferred to occupy ourselves with, but what of the others? I felt obligated to entertain them somehow. I couldn't just assume Bannister, Leroy, Fillmore, and Dresden were on the same wavelength libido-wise. Should we play a game? Was Jenga for six players? I couldn't readily remember. A movie? Television? What did families watch at night to stave off the impending doom of suburban domestic enslavement? Could we escape that rut somehow? I had heard "normal" people watch sitcoms, hour-long dramas, and decadent reality television shows to bond and parrot their regurgitated thoughts at each other. Repetitious gibberish with nary an original thought in their head. Someone once said it was comforting to be able to turn your brain off for a while. How can you appreciate turning your brain off when it's off all the time? It's incredible. But I digress; we settled on an hour-long serialized hospital drama where the characters make big, aggrandizing speeches about life and love and tolerance and acceptance while everyone else listens as heartfelt music drones meekly in the background.

As one outspoken, sassy (because the other characters said she was, repeatedly) nurse or doctor or whoever ramped into a fiery monologue about her fiercely unique autonomy and inflicting it onto everyone within her reach, I could have sworn I saw Fillmore put his hand down Dresden's pants. The sectional sofa we were on seated twelve people comfortably. Or six people regally. It was dark save for the glow of the eighty-five-inch idiot panel we were staring at, but I'm sure I detected motion on the other end of the couch. It was Dresden, then Fillmore, then Bannister, then Leroy, and next to me was Nester. Don't get me wrong, we were jerking each other off underneath the checkerboard microfleece throw blanket we had draped over us, but it was a subtle wank session. No sudden movements or groans. It looked like Fillmore and Dresden were about to embark on a full-on public display of affection, to put it mildly. I looked again, this time not just with my eyes, but with my whole head. I think I might have looked a little too sharply because it caused Fillmore to remove his hand from Dresden's pants with the quickness, making Dresden sigh a little too loud. Instead of saying anything, I just stink-eyed them, which seemed to catch them off-guard. I immediately looked to Bannister and Leroy for support and found them also jerking each other off. They were in my blind spot on the couch, and I hadn't even seen them begin to do so. How long had they been at it, for fuck's sake? The smiles on both their faces said *at least* several minutes as they faded away at my gaze. I knew right then I had made a grave error. Five clones were too much. Much too much.

As the musical montage that signified the end of this episode of television hospital tomfoolery cued up and began to swell, I knew I had to remove myself from the situation. All five of them were looking at me with the same face. My face. But hungry for self-sex. Most likely an unending orgy of self-sex that would kill us all in a sea of orgasmic strokes and seizures.

I grabbed Nester's hand and bade him to leave with me to my (our?) bedroom. It wasn't safe in common spaces anymore. I had a lock on my bedroom door installed when I made the decision to have myself cloned. Right at that very moment I mentally patted myself on the back for such rare forethought. It would keep errant erections from penetrating my (our?) privacy from now on.

What to do? There was obviously no going back out there. At least, not tonight. I would have to make sure Fillmore cleaned the couch thoroughly after what was most likely a four-way me orgy on it. As long as they kept to themselves, I could handle it. We'd have a meeting about expectations going forward in the morning. Hopefully they could at least keep their hands to themselves when not in their bedrooms. That seemed reasonable, right?

Right?

"What was that all about?" Nester asked with more than a little breathy lust in his voice. It didn't sound like me at all. I couldn't tell if I was alarmed or aroused. Or both.

"You saw. You saw what I saw. We can't... I can't control this!"

"...Why would you want to?" Nester was already kneading his rising cock through his (my) camo shorts.

I now realized the true depth of my faux pas. And my current situation. The military was right. This clone shit was for the birds. How can you invade a country when your whipped up army of lookalikes can't stop cumming on each other?

This could only end one of two ways.

An orgy death spiral.

Or...

I had had to, *you know...*

All of them. Preferably sooner rather than later.

But there was still something nagging at the back of my mind.

My libido. It was calling to me and to Nester and somehow, he was picking up on it.

"They can wait. We're in here right now. Just us," he whispered.

A weapon. Any weapon. Why didn't I have a weapon readily available somewhere in my chambers? I thought of the fucking *lock* ahead of time, why couldn't I have thought of a damn weapon?

"Is that all you can think of right now? We can't do it forever. It'll kill us all!"

"And? Is that really so bad?"

"Isn't there anything else you'd like to do? Maybe we can go to the movies or something."

"Cool. Can we fuck there?"

Half of me wanted to bash his brains in right then and there and the other half wanted to fuck his brains out until we both lost consciousness. I had to hand it to United Genetics, Inc. They made a very fuckable clone, no matter how lemming-like their destructive sex drive was.

Nester saw my eyes scanning the room and him being me (mostly) knew right away what I was doing.

"So that's it, huh? One good fuck and I'm food for worms? For crows? What's it then, Daddy?"

Oh Jesus. This was worse than I had ever imagined. Some sort of god/father complex was developing in such a controlled environment. No contact with anyone else but me… Us?

Wait a minute…

Did Leroy ever go to work?

I had never even bothered to ask Dresden if he ran his errands I assigned him for the day.

The house *seemed* clean, but I didn't inspect further than a few cursory glances. Did Fillmore even lift a finger?

How did Bannister manage such a scrumptious dinner on his first night? Unless it was God damn takeout???

I couldn't trust *anything*. Not even myself or my very own urges. Let alone *their* blasted selves or *their* infernal urges.

But I had to put my faith in at least one of them. I was too outnumbered not to at least try.

Then the banging started. On my bedroom door. It sounded like all of them at once trying to get in.

"…You hear that? They're after one thing and one thing only," I said to Nester.

"I know. Isn't that how all this started? Isn't that what you wanted?"

The hurt and confusion in his voice sounded like something I hadn't felt since I was a child. When you realize your parents don't have all the answers. I had to bridge the gap somehow.

BANG BANG BANG BANG

"Look. What we have is great. The best ever. More than I thought it would be. But we can't carry on with them carrying on on top of us. Nothing will ever get done. I should have just cloned one of me. Of you. It would have been easier. Better. I get that now. But I need your help. They have to go." I tried to keep my voice as even-keeled as possible, but it was really hard to do with all that incessant banging happening just feet away. I could hear faint cracks after every other fist pound. They were determined to get in here and I believed it would happen any minute now.

Nester didn't balk at my plea, per se, not outwardly, but he didn't swoon either. He was thinking. Hard. I knew he knew I was right. But those were his… brothers? Out there? Kin of some sort, to be sure. But did he hold any allegiance to them at all? What if he felt pain when they died like they were some sort of oversexed quintuplets forced into adulthood?

We had to find out. At this point, it really seemed like the only way out of this self-induced quagmire.

BANG BANG BANG BANG

"…You want to kill them. Right? And you want me to help. Why? I'm part and parcel with them. How do you know I won't join in and gangfuck you to death as soon as the door is open?"

"Because I'm trusting you. I picked you for a reason. I felt something when I saw you in that lineup, dressed in my old clothes. Our clothes. It's gotta mean something."

The word trust seemed to seal the deal for Nester. His body language changed. He moved a little closer to me. His breathing quickened slightly.

BANG BANG BANG CRRRACK

I could see part of a fist make its way through the wooden door to my bedroom. Our bedroom? Bloody, bruised, cut up. They were killing themselves to get in here. We had to act now.

"This is it. When they're through, all bets are off. There's no telling what they'll do to us or for how long. I don't have that kind of endurance. Not after earlier today. Do you?"

"…Not really. No."

"Good. It's settled. We kill them and then we can be together. That's what you want, right?"

"Is that what you want?"

"…Sure."

"Then that's what I want, too."

"Great. Find a weapon. Something. Anything."

We both scanned the room in a mild panic, looking for whatever phallic instrument, whether blunt or sharp, happened to lurk within. We were coming up zero so far.

"You check my desk. I'll look in the bathroom," I whispered to Nester as another fist broke through the quickly failing door. I could feel my heart racing now, too. And not in the way I wanted when I initially set this whole clusterfuck in motion.

Nester nodded and bounded over to my computer desk, ripping open drawers on both sides, rifling through everything all at once.

I dashed to my private bathroom on the other side of my (our?) room and stood in the threshold, hoping to see something conveniently placed there for just such an occasion.

And what occasion would that be? Unaliving five sex doppelgangers?

The plunger would have to do. It was literally the only thing in there that even remotely resembled a weapon. I didn't have the proper training to make toenail clippers lethal to anyone.

"Got it!" Nester gasped from my bedroom.

I popped my head back out and saw him dual-wielding screwdrivers. One Phillips-head and one flathead. About eight inches each. Perfect for stabbing eyes. I don't remember ever using either one. Or what I would even buy them for. Kebabs?

"Perfect for stabbing eyes," I said out loud involuntarily.

"Y-Yeah… O…okay," Nester stuttered, knowing it was true but not expecting such a flavor of directness.

The next few door bangs brought with it the clatter of large wooden splinters to the floor. It was all about to happen.

I made my way to just a foot from the buckling door, plunger in hand. I looked to Nester, hoping to see some sort of resolve on his face. There was a little there. I think.

"Ready?"

He just nodded. That meant he was more ready than I was. Inspiring.

"We just want to talk!" Dresden's voice came amidst the uproar.

Sure. Talk. I "talked" with Nester for hours earlier.

That gave me an idea, though.

"Okay, let's talk."

The commotion died down a little and Dresden poked his me of a head through the massive hole in the door.

Opportunity achieved.

I took the non-business end of my plunger and jammed it right down Dresden's gullet, impaling him with a virtually dull wooden stake. I jammed and jammed and jammed until gouts of blood spurted out around the sides of his mouth. I must have hit his stomach instead of his lungs because the foul stench of pungent stomach acid invaded my nostrils. It almost made me puke right in Dresden's face. The others seemed to be in shock, apparently too horny and surprised to calculate any possible outcome of this nature. They were cockblind. Cumwashed. I can't say I haven't been there.

I yanked the plunger out of Dresden's maw, flipped it around to plunge mode, and shoved him off and out onto the floor outside. His blood-caked head made a surprisingly high-pitched clunk.

Bannister was next through the door, visibly outraged. I guess there was no more wiggle room for negotiations at this point.

Nester was on him with an intimidating scream of fear and anger. Both of Bannister's eyes became host to a pair of screwdrivers in mere seconds. Nester had pushed them in so hard and so fast, Bannister's eyeballs folded like they were nothing as the tips of the screwdrivers punched through the back of his head, twin spurts of eye pus and brain matter squeezed through the puncture holes as Nester unsheathed the tools from said head just as quickly as they went in.

Bannister's exit gave Leroy and Fillmore pause. A big fucking pause. And then they ran away. Scampered to another part of the house. It very much sounded like they had separated. Why they didn't leave through the front door still remains a mystery to me even now.

Nester and I exchanged glances and just nodded at each other. We knew the score.

Two down, two to go.

"I got Fillmore," Nester said with barely caught breath.

"Leroy it is," I replied, twirling my plunger between my fingers and winking at Nester.

Now felt like a good time for a kiss for good luck, or whatever they do in the movies when two characters are about to split up. I guess Nester felt the same way because he grabbed me around the waist and laid one on me. I can't lie, it was hot. I was a good kisser and getting kissed by someone who was made from someone who's a good kisser was a next-level experience.

He ended our kiss and looked right into my eyes as he said, "Be careful."

"You too," I said, and I think I was grinning as I did so. Felt like I was.

I unlocked the door from the inside and swung the dilapidated, defeated door open. Pieces of it fell to the ground as it creaked around to fully ajar. Dresden and Bannister lay within *and* just without the door frame, decidedly dead. No twitches, no gurgles. Nothing remained. Job well done on both our accounts. Time to finish it.

I rushed to the foot of the stairs leading upwards. I looked back for Nester as he headed to the kitchen with purpose. He had this well in hand. It looked like he was gripping those screwdrivers with an iron vice just underneath his skin. It made me wince. I felt for Fillmore a bit. Almost. As I bounded up the stairs, I could hear sobbing. In one of the bedrooms. Down the hall. The door was shut about halfway. Incessant sobbing. Leroy. At least I thought it was him. It's definitely *me*, whoever it is.

As I closed the distance in the hallway between myself and the door, the sobbing stopped. Was this a trap? Or the unraveling of a defective, blue-balled replicant? Either way, I had to be resolute. No hesitation. Go for the plunge straight away.

I pushed the half-open door all the way open with a gentle foot, clutching my plunger in both hands like a spear, ready to perform a Dresden on whoever lay in wait.

As the door cleared fully and I took in the whole room, I could see a naked me standing with their back to me, staring out the window into the thick forest surrounding my property. No more sobbing. I could tell he was jerking off, though. But there was no passion to it. Just robotic masturbation. Is that how I looked when I did it? It was unnerving to say the least.

"…Leroy?"

"…Will it hurt?" He asked me.

"Probably. It's a blunt wooden stick attached to a hard rubber suction cup."

"Would… Would you kill me with the rubber side?"

"Uh, that would take an awful long time."

"I… I know. What else have I got to do? Just wanted to cum inside you, Father. And you in me. Is that too much to ask?"

"I decide who gets fucked and when. You had one job to do. One. Job. Is *that* too much to ask?"

He had no answer. I honestly felt kind of terrible. I was yelling at a naked version of myself who only wanted love. No. It was lust. Same thing though, I think.

"Any theories on what happens when we die?"

Oh no. *That* question. I could say a lot of things. How I believed we just go back to the way it was before we were born. The silent peace of non-existence. Only the vain and selfish could be afraid of such a thing. Maybe that could comfort him before I performed murder directly his way?

Instead, I just said "Not really."

Leroy finally turned to face me as he started ejaculating all over the floor. Dehydrated, gelatinous spunk pitter-patted on the hardwood floor of my parent's old bedroom. I wondered what they would have thought of this particular scenario as he shivered the last bit of orgasm out of his body.

"Make it last a while so I can remember your face."

Instead of reminding him we had the same boring visage, I just said "Sure," and immediately went about beating him to death with the soft side of my plunger. It took forever. A good fifteen minutes. He sobbed for the first five as I tried to break his head skin effectively and then nothing. Just labored breathing. He never tried to fight back. Half an erection throughout the whole ordeal, even well after I had cracked into bone and began mashing up his brains. It made me sick all down the hallway back toward the stairs. His erection, not the head trauma.

After catching my breath and wiping puke from my face at the top of the staircase, I trudged down the stairs proper. Grunting came from the kitchen. Was the struggle still on? Had Nester found Fillmore and tried to reason with him, resulting in a protracted confrontation?

As I made it to the entrance to the kitchen, I realized that was not the case whatsoever.

They were fucking.

Fillmore was completely naked and had Nester's shorts and boxers down around his ankles, railing him right on the floor from behind harder than I ever did to Nester during our lovemaking session. Was that jealousy I was feeling? All I could see was red as I spotted the butane torch on the kitchen counter that Bannister had planned to use to flambé some meringue for tomorrow night's dessert. Those plans were decidedly canceled now, and I felt that taking the torch and grabbing Fillmore by the scruff of his head of hair and melting off his tongue with that very same torch was the best course of action.

So I did just that.

I held his head back firmly so as to ensure he choked on his own melting tongue as he blew his load inside Nester. I unloaded the rest of the torch's flames in Fillmore's face and his screams sounded a lot like my screams. Or maybe it was me screaming instead of him. Did it matter at that point? It was me screaming regardless of the body it came from.

I used my trusty plunger like a lever and hoisted Fillmore off Nester with a wet pop. Nester shit himself from the force of the suction and I couldn't help but laugh.

"That's not funny. What took you so long?"

"Was he raping you?"

"No, I uh, thought it would be easier to distract him with sex since that's all that we, I mean they, care about. You know?"

"Great plan. How long were you planning on waiting for me? What if Leroy killed me?"

"I knew that wouldn't happen."

"How?"

"Is it over?"

"Yeah. It's done."

"Did he suffer?"

"Probably way too much. But he wanted it that way."

"I think we're designed like that."

"…What?"

He just stood there, staring at me, shit caking his legs.

"Howsabout we clean that up?" I offer.

"Oh, yeah. Thanks."

I helped him to my (our?) bathroom and shower with him, decisively getting rid of all the blood and shit we had accumulated. I let him wear my (our?) bathrobe and I threw on a pair of gym shorts and a ratty old t-shirt. We had a quiet early breakfast as the sun came up. I could smell my clones deteriorating throughout the house. It made our meager meal of English muffins with strawberry jam and margarine and Frosted Mini Wheats completely unmemorable.

"…So, what do you want to do?" Nester asked me.

I don't remember when exactly during our fuck session I decided Nester had to go, too, but it was definitely after I had blown my own load and before he had a chance to do the same. Don't get me wrong, it was great, but nothing was so great as to ignore the mounting problems my houseguests had contributed to since we all arrived as one happy family at my abode. The psychic feeling in my member when I was giving him pleasure had died down considerably since we last fucked. That was more than a little disappointing to say the least.

His screwdrivers went right into his eye sockets and my plunger went down his gullet. The rubber end. It ripped through his lips and knocked out his teeth and tore apart his esophagus, but it went down. After several attempts. I didn't even think to make sure his cock was out of my ass when he died. My arms were on fire from reaching around to insert my implements of destruction into his moaning visage. There was no sobbing from him. I think he was trying to finish even while he knew he was dying.

I think he tried to say "I love you" to me as he drew his last breath.

And so, I said "I love you too," just in case.

*   *   *

So here I am. On hold with a lovely young Pakistani woman named Gennifer. I've been on hold with her so long that I got her to tell me her real name. It's Suni. Very pretty. She claims she's part of a very busy call center, but I've called and hung up on her seven times in a row and gotten only her on every single attempt. So, I assume United

146

Genetics, Inc. has one of those high-tech Suni call centers. Very efficient. She says she sympathizes with my situation. She says she's dealt with this before. I believe her. But it doesn't make Nester's dick in my ass any less soft. They say hard-ons don't go away in death and I believe it now. Every time I move it feels like a load is getting pumped into me. And so, I just sit here, on hold with Suni.

The battery on my phone is at 37%. I hate that number. Thirty-seven. It's a shitty, stupid number. Lowly, but not too lowly to panic over. An insignificant existence for a number.

Fuck.

I ask Suni how much longer until I can speak with a licensed genetics disposal specialist. She says about another fifteen minutes. They're dealing with another situation at the moment.

I wonder what it could be. Could be anything. Maybe it's weirder than my issue. Maybe my issue is standard as fuck? Boring bullshit. What if Suni's bored with me? Maybe I'm the third asshole with his fifth clone's dick inside him?

I shudder at feeling banal even though the odds are that I indeed am. We all are, most likely. Well, at least most of us.

She asks me to locate the serial number of replicant #005 before putting me on hold.

I'm pretty sure it's on his dick.

Which is in my ass currently.

I twist my body to try and see if I can spy the barcode and serial number on the top of his dick. I can barely make it out as my back muscles begin to cramp and spasm.

Another one of Nester's loads ejects into my ass.

This is going to be a long fucking call.

36%

I sigh loudly, even though no one on either side of the line can hear me. It makes me feel better, though.

I really hope the next batch is easier to control.

NOTES

Well, I have no idea about this one. Your guess is as good as mine. This is an original in every sense of the word. Technically, I had it in mind for an anthology call and I just never got past the first few hundred words. Those first few hundred are a doozy, but a story they do not make. The word requirement for that open call was 4000 and this one ended up well over 6000 so that idea went out the fucking window in a hurry. I felt it would be perfect to end this collection with a bang, in more ways than one. One of my favorite movies that no one seems to care about is Harold Ramis' *Multiplicity*, where a guy clones himself a bunch of times and they all develop their own personalities. As funny as the movie objectively is, I felt it wasn't horny enough. I'd like to think this piece has been in my head in some way, shape, or form since the summer of 1996. I think this story says more about my opinion (or lack thereof) of humans as a species and my thoughts on existence itself more than anything as banal as my own personal sexuality or relationship history. Yeah. I mean, this story collection is called *The Comfy-Cozy Nihilist* and not *Chicken Soup for the Fuckheaded Soul*. Sleep tight.

OUTRO...

"Wait. What? You need a fucking epilogue for your dumb story collection, too?"

Yeah. I do. I put a lot of work into this thing, and you should check out my final thoughts.

If you've made it this far (congrats, by the way) then you already know that having a sense of humor helps out a whole hell of a lot when faced with such utter darkness in this world. What else is there to do if you don't want to kill yourself? As much as I detest humans in the macro sense, I've grown accustomed to a lot of cool things in this world.

But you fell in love. Got married. Had kids. How can you want all that and still be a nihilist?

...A misanthrope?

Well, dear reader, humans are fucking complicated. And as I said, I've grown attached to things in this corporeal existence. What other explanation do you need?

One of my favorite movies is *Sound of Noise*. A Swedish film from 2011 about a group of anarchist "criminals" who burst into various social situations and perform impromptu concerts with whatever is laying around in said situation. Once such example is when they bust in on a man receiving open heart surgery and the misfits jam out with the surgical equipment and the machines documenting the man's vital signs. Oh, and a tone-def cop who hates music is the one trying to catch them. It is a joyously bizarre and hilarious film that makes my heart happy. There's hardly any violence or edginess or profanity to be had. But that's not the point. The artistry on display – the sheer filmmaking – is beyond most people's abilities. It speaks of talent that is ethereal and inspiring in the most primordial sense. The first time I saw the film was the hardest I've laughed and smiled and cried tears of happiness in a long time. And then I promptly turned around and wrote a dark and violent screenplay about wendigos, serial cannibals, and clinically depressed federal agents who can raise the dead.

People are fucking complicated, man. And inspiration comes from the strangest of places.

So just make yourself as comfortable as possible until oblivion takes you. Make art. Fall in love. Eat good food. Masturbate and fuck in weird places. And if you're lucky, you'll be comfy for a while.

Hope to see you around.

ACKNOWLEDGEMENTS...

Thank you to the following amazing human beings who have inspired me in some way, shape, or form over the last several years.

Mary-Colleen Millage, Raygan Ketterer, Chad Farmer, Jessica Farmer, Samantha Kolesnik, Mike Lombardo, Jeff Frumess, Zane Hershberger, Nic Champeaux, Daniel Cordery, John Hale, Jeffrey Howe, Lex Quinn, Jeremy Herbert, Ryan LaPlante, Mark Towse, Waylon Jordan, Dawn Shea, Cody Langille, Michael Evans, Harrison Graves, Todd Densmore, Ryan Imhoff, Evan Baughfman, Jaysen Buterin, Diana Woody, Aaron Barrocas, Jamal Hodge, Rafael De Leon Jr., Rakefet Abergel, Roy Frumkes, Brian W. Smith, Vincent Vinas, Jonathan Straiton, Brie Straiton, Landon Knoblock, Michael Merchant, Brett Janeski, Ryan Felker, Tim Troemner, Saba, Greg Sisco, Timothy Troy, Tim Vester, Morgan McLeod, JoAnn Hess, Virginia Shine, Paul Grammatico, Wendy Keeling, Chris Warner and Bryan L. Nuri.

Special thanks to Corrina Morse, Christina Pfeiffer, Dakota Dawe, Diana Richie, Donna Latham, Mark Robinson, Jason Nickey, Robert Whiting, Terry Miller, RJ Benetti, and Mark MJ Green. Your reviews and support for this new author and their first book are more appreciated than you'll ever know.

And an extra special thank you to Gerri & Roy Ludwig, aka Mom & Dad, for deciding to bake me in the ol' oven. You raised me quite right indeed.

ABOUT THE AUTHOR...

Nathan is an author, award-winning screenwriter, average filmmaker, and decent producer. His debut novel, *Love Potion #666*, is available via D&T Publishing. Be on the lookout for his next books coming soon: *Method Hack, The Resurrection Girl, Sacrificial Wolves,* and *The*

Tartarus Contract. He is currently co-writing a novel with Chad Farmer entitled *Love, Post-Mortem.*

Nathan has co-directed of a handful of short films with Chad Farmer; *Late Submission, PMS: Pre-teen Monster Syndrome, The Big D*, and *What's for Dinner*? But wait. There's more. He's the director and founder of the GenreBlast Film Festival, a top genre fest in the world emanating from the Alamo Drafthouse Cinema in Winchester, VA. He's also the producer of feature film *Worst Laid Plans* along with his producing partner Samantha Kolesnik.

Nathan is a two-service military veteran and a Libra. He resides just outside Richmond, VA with his wife Mary-Colleen and their two ridiculously perfect-as-hell daughters Georgie and Charleigh. Check out The Reel '96 Podcast where he does a deep dive into every film from 1996. It's definitely a thing.

On Instagram and Twitter, find him @loogenhausen. On TikTok he lurks at nathan.d.ludwig.